"You're Touching Me," Cami Said

"That's not allow

Rafe's fingers tig
in his dark eyes.

"It all depends on
He reached out and took up the handcuffs, then turned to her with a glint in his eyes. "I'm going to have to put the cuffs back on you."

She shrank back. "No!"

"You tried to make a break for it, lady. You're not cooperating like a suspected criminal should."

"I'm sorry I did that," she said, backing away. "I won't do it again. Honest."

Rafe hesitated. She was saying the right words, but the look in her eyes told him she was feeling anything but meek. Still, what was he going to do, tie her up?

At the thought of that, a part of him cringed. She was so pretty, so…

No. What was the matter with him? He was a cop. He'd locked up prettier women than this. And he was going to do the same here.

But not yet…

Dear Reader,

It's the moment you've all been waiting for, the publication of the 1000th Silhouette Desire®. It's Diana Palmer's *Connal*, the next title in her terrific TEXAN LOVERS mini-series. Diana was one of the very first Desire writers, and her many wonderful contributions to the line have made her one of our most beloved authors. This story is sure to make its way to your shelf of 'keepers'.

And there's so much more! Don't miss *Baby Dreams*, the first book in a fabulous new series, THE BABY SHOWER, by Raye Morgan. Award-winning author Jennifer Greene also starts a new mini-series, THE STANFORD SISTERS, with the delightful *The Unwilling Bride*. For something a little different, take a peek at Joan Elliott Pickart's *Apache Dream Bride*. And the fun keeps on coming with Judith McWilliams' *Instant Husband*, the second in THE WEDDING NIGHT series. Last, but by no means least, we've got promising new author Amanda Kramer's charming and sexy *Baby Bonus*.

What a line-up! And that's not all, because if you turn to the end pages you'll find your chance to win a year's worth of Silhouette Desire novels—absolutely FREE! We know you'll enjoy our celebration month. Long may the passion continue!

Sincerely,

The Editors

Baby Dreams

RAYE MORGAN

SILHOUETTE

Desire®

*Silhouette, Silhouette Desire and Colophon
are registered trademarks of Harlequin Books S.A.,
used under licence.*

*First published in Great Britain 1996
Silhouette Books, Eton House, 18-24 Paradise Road,
Richmond, Surrey TW9 1SR*

© Helen Conrad 1996

ISBN 0 373 75997 5

22-9610

*Printed and bound in Great Britain
by Mackays of Chatham PLC, Chatham*

RAYE MORGAN

favours settings in the West, which is where she has spent most of her life. She admits to a penchant for Western heroes, believing that whether he's a rugged outdoorsman or a smooth city sophisticate, he tends to have a streak of wildness that the romantic heroine can't resist taming. She's been married to one of those Western men for twenty years and is busy raising four more in her Southern California home.

Other Silhouette® Books by Raye Morgan

Silhouette Desire®

Embers of the Sun
Summer Wind
Crystal Blue Horizon
A Lucky Streak
Husband for Hire
Too Many Babies
Ladies' Man
In a Marrying Mood
Baby Aboard
Almost a Bride
The Bachelor
Caution: Charm at Work
Yesterday's Outlaw
The Daddy Due Date
Babies on the Doorstep
Sorry, the Bride Has Escaped

Dear Reader,

What an anniversary! One thousand Silhouette Desire novels. One thousand red books, packed full of love, laughter and touching moments. Do you have them all? I have a friend who does—all those red books in a row on a special set of shelves her husband built for her in her bedroom wardrobe. Any time she wants, she can pick one out and recall the surprises, the sudden laughs out loud, the tears, the sighs.

That's what romance is all about—emotions. Who doesn't like to think about what it feels like to fall in love—to see that special guy for the first time...the thrill the first time he touches you...the first time he kisses you.... In real life you usually only get to fall in love once. Between the covers of those red books, you could have done it one thousand times! And I get to go even further—I get to write them (well, not all thousand).

Thank you for reading them. Thank you for loving them. This anniversary is for all of us to celebrate. Happy birthday, Silhouette Desire!

Love to you all,

Raye Morgan

Prologue

The Invitation

"*R*eginald, my darling, don't you understand? I'm about to have... I mean, I'm...oh dear, it's just that...don't you see? Can't you tell?"

"Margaret, my precious one, you're not... I say, you can't mean...that is, you're not saying that you..."

"Yes! Oh, my love, it's true! We'll need a new wing on the old mansion."

"Oh, my dearest. You've made me the happiest man in the world. At last, our love will be complete."

"Yes, Reginald. At last. At long, long, last."

The music in the soundtrack swelled with triumph and joy as "The End" swept across the screen, and Cami Bishop reached for another handkerchief at the same time she switched off the TV with the remote. She sniffed as she dabbed at her eyes. Looking around the nest she'd made for herself while watching the old movie, she noticed there were far too many used tissues littering the couch. Even for a rainy Saturday, this was a bit too much.

Listening to the early spring rain on the roof while sitting around in her pajamas and sobbing over happy endings was a guilty pleasure she only indulged in on days like this. There was just something about people falling in love and having babies that sent her into orbit.

"Maybe," she noted dryly to herself, "that's because it seems more and more like fantasy, something that could never happen to me."

Once, it had seemed a sure thing. She'd wasted years on a relationship that had evaporated when she'd finally tried to pin it down. Now she felt like someone running for a bus that was picking up speed and pulling away.

But self-pity wasn't her style, and she brushed away maudlin thoughts, pulling back her thick, curling blond hair and shoving a band around it, keeping it out of her eyes while she steeled herself to fight off the wave of weariness that seemed to be tugging at her senses.

The sound of her mail delivery hitting the floor of her entryway brought a quick surge of relief. At last, something to think about besides the babies that she would probably never have.

Jumping up, she padded to the door in her panda bear slippers and bent to retrieve the stack of magazines and envelopes.

"A bill from the phone company, a bill from the department store, a magazine on organic gardening, a flyer from my dentist . . ."

And then, a pink envelope with no return address, but heavily scented with a familiar smell. What was that? Baby powder? She held the envelope for a moment, feeling the texture of the linen paper in her hand. Then, holding it up to her hall light to see the shape of the card inside, she reveled in anticipation.

What could it be? An announcement of some sort? An invitation?

Her heart was beating just a little faster than it had a moment before. This was going to be something good. She could feel it. This was going to change her life.

"Yes!" she said under her breath. "Whatever it is, yes!"

Quickly she grabbed her letter opener and made a slit along the top of the envelope. The card that fell out was shaped like a cunning duck, wearing a tiny pink satin bow at his throat and holding a frilly umbrella. "A Baby Shower" the caption read. "We're excited, 'cuz you're definitely invited!"

Cami's heart fell, along with her shoulders. "No," she groaned, closing her eyes for a moment. "Not another baby shower."

Was everyone in the country having babies except for her?

Flipping open the card, she braced herself. "Come help welcome a new little person," the card read. Her gaze slipped down to the handwritten note at the bottom of the page. "You'll notice there's no phone number for an RSVP. That's because you *will* be here. Excuses are not an option. Cami, I'm dying to see you. Eight years is too long."

Sara Parker. Her college roommate. Despite everything, a smile curled Cami's wide, generous mouth. Turning to her desk, she rummaged in a drawer and pulled out a framed picture of four young women smiling at the camera, their faces full of hope.

Sara and Hailey and J.J.... and Cami herself. So young. The Fab Four, they'd called themselves. It seemed like yesterday, and yet...so much had happened since then. That youthful optimism was hard to muster up lately.

And now Sara was going to be the first of their group to have a baby. Cami couldn't help but feel a twinge at that news. Back in the old days, Cami had been the one who had been full of dreams of romance and making a family. The others had laughed at her. They'd all had other goals—careers, travel, adventure. Hailey was going to study art in Paris. J.J. planned a career in journalism. Sara was going to take over her father's business—and then she was going to marry someone with the potential for real glory—maybe even the future president—they'd all said so. Smart and elegant, she'd make the perfect First Lady. And now, here she was having a baby shower.

Cami looked down at her wrinkled pajamas and her panda bear slippers and sighed. It wasn't that she was a failure. After all, she was busy publishing and editing a successful specialty magazine, and doing a darn good job of it, if she did say so herself. Still, there was no longer a man in her life—hadn't been for ages.

"Maybe there never will be," she whispered, looking about at her lonely home. No husband. No babies. She was thirty. Was this it? Had she missed her chance? Would there never be a Reginald in her life?

"Oh, grow up!" she told herself disgustedly. "There is no Reginald, you dreamer. Face reality. Life and romance just don't mix, not in the real world."

There. That settled it. She needed one of these little pep talks every now and then. But at the same time, she was happy for her friend—her best friend. And full of resolve.

Yes, she would go to the baby shower. She was only human, and it wouldn't be easy, seeing Sara's happiness when she felt so left out. But she would do it. She had to.

The address on the card told her Sara was still living in Denver. She would drive there, she decided quickly. And suddenly she was *filled* with excitement. To see Sara again, and to maybe even see her new baby—that was going to be special. She could hardly wait.

Now what was she going to wear? Panda slippers were out. If she was going to portray an image of success and competence, she would need a new wardrobe. Gee, what a shame!

One

The snow was going to get bad. There was no way around it. It was fixing to storm. By midnight, the roads would be impassable. If he wanted to take one last run up the mountain, he'd best get to it.

Rafe Lonewolf strapped on his holster and put his service revolver in place, then shrugged into his heavy down jacket, pushed his hat onto his head and stepped out into the icy wind, heading for his blue-and-white unit.

A silver sedan was passing. It slowed to a stop and the window rolled down.

"Hey, good-lookin'," called out the pretty young woman in the driver's seat. A ruff of fur framed her face, just showing a hint of the long, black braid that was coiled at the crown of her head. Slanted dark eyes gave her an exotic look. "Want to come over for some hot coffee before you go?"

"No thanks, Sally," he called, pausing and rocking back on his heels to nod to her. "I'm just going to make a run up to the ridge to make sure the Santos place is locked up for the night. I've only got one more hour on duty. Then I'm going to turn in.''

"Okay," she said, smiling at him playfully. "Then come on over after you get back. It's going to be a cold night. You're going to need something to warm you up." Her mischievous eyes sparkled, telling him she had more than coffee in mind.

He paused, kicking the heel of his cowboy boot against the curb, then sauntered to the car and looked down at her. "Sally, honey," he said ruefully, giving her a slow, wry grin. "Give it up. What do you want with an old man like me, anyway?"

"You're not an old man," she said, looking slightly horrified.

His mouth twisted. "I'm charging hard toward forty, and you know it. You can't be more than nineteen. You've got every young buck in the county crazy about you. Choose one of them."

She pouted prettily. "Sometimes a girl hankers for a man with experience," she told him, her gaze still flirtatious. "Sometimes those guys just seem so young."

He laughed. "Pick a young one, Sally. He's liable to be more trainable. This old experienced male is a little too far-gone for you."

She shrugged, still hopeful, and bit her lip teasingly. "Maybe you just need something special to recharge your batteries."

He laughed again, drawing back. "No, I'd have to have a complete overhaul to deal with a bright young thing like you. Face it, Sally. I'm just an old bachelor, too set in my ways to change."

Sally sighed and shook her head, still smiling. "I'm just talking about one evening, Sheriff. I'm not asking you to marry me."

Not yet, anyway. But he only thought that, didn't say it aloud. It was his experience that women always came around to the marriage thing, no matter how much they protested along the way—almost as though it were something implanted in their blood, something they couldn't help—any more than he could help his aversion to it.

"Sam says you've got a tragic love affair in your past," she said, not ready to give up at all. "Is he right?"

He wasn't prepared for that, and whenever anyone blindsided him with the subject, it always took a second or two to steady himself. For a fraction of time, a picture of Janie flashed into his mind. It was more than a picture, really. There was the scent of gunpowder, the sting as one of the bullets crashed deep into the muscle of his thigh, the sound of Janie's soft cry, the red haze of blood that spattered as she fell. And then he closed it off again. He always did. He never thought about Janie in front of people. He saved that for when he was alone.

"Sorry," he said, shaking his head. "Nothing that romantic." Grinning, he gave her car a slap. "Get on home. A storm's coming up."

She gave him one last smile, full of regret, and took off toward her house. Rafe chuckled as he walked on over and got into his car. There was no way he would ever touch that girl, but he had to admit, her little crush on him was good for the old ego.

The tires crunched on the new-fallen snow, and he knew when he got up a little higher, the precipitation was really going to get thick. Good thing he still had on his snow tires. This late in the season, he hadn't expected another storm before the full spring thaw. But even snow tires were not going to take him all the way to the Santos place if he didn't hurry.

Turning up toward the mountain, he traveled quickly on a road that hadn't seen many cars that day. Three years in this area and he still wasn't used to it—the peace—the wonderful peace. It was the ultimate contrast to the rest of his life. Down in Los Angeles, he'd been a cop in a department under siege—the gang fights, the drive-by shootings, the hatred, the resentments.

There was no hatred up here in Clear Creek. Not that things were perfect. But here, people dealt with each other one-on-one, with some understanding, some willingness to compromise. No one was staking out territory. It was a brand-new world for him, a world he had grown to love. Sure, compared to L.A., it was boring. And that was the way he liked it.

His car climbed high on the winding mountain road and he checked out the Santos place, securing locks on the gates, then started back down, anticipating his bed. Just as he came to the crossroads, something caught his eye—a light, high up on the old forest road.

"Damn," he breathed, watching it as it moved. Someone was up there, and that road was closed. It looked as if he weren't going to make it home as quickly as he'd thought. In fact, he might just be looking at a very long night.

Turning his car back up, he headed toward the gate-crasher, and his mood was less than cheery.

She was lost. It had to be near midnight and the snow was getting worse. And she was lost.

This was crazy. She was crazy. Who expected snow this close to spring? But why had she taken that shortcut, anyway? Here she was in the mountains of New Mexico, looking for angles, just like always.

And getting in trouble because of it. That was just like always, too.

What on earth was she doing out here in the wilderness, anyway? She was a city girl, born and bred. She knew all there was to know about navigating the freeways and alleyways of Southern California. She knew very little about icy mountain roads.

She hadn't seen another car for an hour. For all she knew, she'd driven right out of civilization and into the twilight zone. She let out a small shriek as the car skidded and came to rest turned broadside. Her pulse was beating like a drum as she straightened out her car. Was she going to have to pull over and wait for morning?

Her heart lurched as lights appeared in her rearview mirror. Another human being! Hallelujah.

But then a red light began to flash behind her. The cops. She groaned, half laughing. Every bit of good news had bad news tacked onto it tonight. If he was going to give her a ticket out here in the middle of nowhere...

She pulled over and turned off her engine, sighing, then watched in her mirror as he slowly got out of the police car behind her, holding on to his hat as a vicious gust of wind tried to take it. He looked big and grouchy. Just her luck.

"Hello, Officer," she said brightly, rolling down her window as he approached the driver's side of the car. She winced as snowflakes hit her nose with a sting. "I can't tell you how happy I am to see a friendly face. Where am I, anyway?"

Ignoring the question, his dark eyes made a quick inventory of the interior of her car. "Where do you think you're going?" he asked, all business.

She hesitated. On this road? Absolutely nowhere. "To a baby shower in Denver," she said aloud. "Am I going the wrong way?"

Something about the set of his chin told her she wasn't going to get an answer to that question.

"May I see your license, please?" he intoned evenly.

She swallowed. Not a ticket, on top of everything else. "What was I doing?" she asked, putting off the inevitable.

His dark face didn't respond in kind to her friendly smile, but he did tell her what he thought. "Driving like an idiot," he noted calmly.

Her smile became a little more strained. "Have they got a special number in the vehicle code for that now?"

His bland look darkened into a frown. Obviously he wasn't in the mood for light repartee. "Let me see your license, please," he repeated, his voice just a shade more steely.

"Okay." She sighed, resigned. "My license." She reached onto the floor beside her seat where she always kept her purse. Her hand didn't contact anything familiar. "Just a second." She reached under the seat, then looked behind it. A tiny flare of panic began to lick at her throat. Where the heck was her purse?

"Wait a minute. I can't find my purse," she said.

"Interesting," he murmured dryly.

She glanced at him, caught by something in his tone. "No, really, I have it. It's here somewhere."

But she still couldn't find it. Oh, brother. Now what? She thought back quickly. She'd made a stop about three miles ago when the snow had begun to blind her. She'd taken out her map to see if she was on the right road, then had gone back to the trunk to see if there were any chains hiding there. At one point, she'd thought she sensed something falling out into the swirling snow, but when she'd looked she hadn't seen it again. Now she knew—it must have been her purse falling out of the car.

She gasped. "Oh, my God. I must have knocked it out along the road back about three miles," she told him. Twisting, she looked at the darkened road and had a quick flashback to a child's fairy tale, complete with witches and goblins hiding in the shapes of trees. "I . . . I'll have to run back and take a look."

His face didn't change. "No," he said firmly.

She blinked at his impassive look. She wasn't used to this kind of unsympathetic opposition. It did tend to put her back up.

"What do you mean, no? My purse is back there. Someone might pick it up. All my money and my credit cards are in there."

The cynical glint in his dark eyes deepened. "Listen, lady," he said evenly. "Don't bother to try a con on me. I've heard them all."

A con? She almost smiled. She was the last person to try to con anyone. Most of her friends thought she was much too open and forthright as it was. But she kind of liked being thought of as a latent con artist. Still, this was the police. She probably ought to take him seriously.

"Well, I can't prove who I am," she told him brightly, pushing back her thick, curly hair with a casual motion that came to her naturally...and often. "But I can tell you, and you're just going to have to take my word for it. Cami Bishop, from Marina Del Rey, California."

His mouth twisted. He'd obviously noted her pushing back her hair and thought it an affectation that might even border on flirting. The set of his mouth told her he didn't succumb to flirting. "A swinging California single, no doubt," he said, almost sneering.

She squinted, trying to see him better. In the dark, with his hat pulled down low, all she could really make out was a hard mouth cut like a slash in granite and a pair of dark eyes that were colder than the icy wind that was making periodic raids on their position. She hesitated. Something about this man could give a girl chills.

"That's a bit of an exaggeration," she said, then tried one last grin. "But basically, yes." And even at that, she couldn't get a smile out of him. Oh well. "Anyway, I'm on my way to this baby shower..."

"Hold it." Cocking his hat back, he stared at her for a long moment, then drew away from her window abruptly, as though he'd just thought of something, something that startled him.

"What?" She blinked at him, surprised.

"Just hold on," he told her sternly. "I'll get back to you."

Rolling up her window to keep the snow out, she lifted her gaze to the rearview mirror to watch him walk to his patrol car, stamping his boots to clear a path. Why did these guys always seem to swagger? She supposed it was meant to make peons like her stay in line. Too bad. Lines and boundaries had never been her forte.

In a moment, he was back, and she only rolled down the window a crack this time. After all, there was a limit to the amount of snow she was going to let the wind whip in around her. It was freezing and she had no heavy coat.

Why she'd left Santa Fe in only this medium-weight linen suit was a question she would be asking herself later on, along with many others—such as, what sort of an idiot had she been to brave the mountains on a night like this? But that was all waiting for the moment when this trip was over and she would have the luxury of second thoughts and incredulous comments. For now, basic survival seemed more important.

"Get out of the car," he said, his voice hard and authoritative.

"What?" She squinted, trying to see him better. He sounded meaner than before. And here she'd been hoping for a thaw in their relationship. "It's snowing!"

"Get out of the car," he ordered grimly, "face it, and spread your arms out."

And that was when she noticed he had his gun drawn.

Her heart leapt into her throat. Suddenly things seemed very serious indeed. "What are you doing?" she gasped, staring down the black muzzle of the weapon.

"Get out of the car, face it, and spread your arms out."

She swallowed hard. He had a bad habit of repeating himself, but she wasn't about to call him on it now. For one split second, she considered starting up her engine and driving off as though all this had never happened. But that gun was just too ominous. And the snow was just too heavy. And most of all, his face was just too hard and cold.

"Okay," she said hoarsely. "Just a minute. I'm getting out."

She put her hands up so he could see she had nothing in them. Wasn't that what they always did on TV? Then she stepped out, her soft leather shoes sliding a bit on the sleet-covered blacktop. She looked at him questioningly, shivering with the cold, and he gestured for her to turn.

"Spread your arms," he said softly, but his softer tone seemed even more chilling and she complied quickly, gasping again as he stepped up close behind her and reached out to pat down her sides.

"This is insane," she said sharply, pulling away from his touch.

"Hold still," he ordered, taking control of her by the back of the neck the way a cat might a kitten. "And listen carefully to your rights. You have the right to remain silent . . ."

She shook her head slowly as he went down the list he was obliged to give her. He was arresting her. This was surreal. It couldn't be happening. She'd just been driving along, on her way to Denver to see old friends and have a jolly time celebrating her college roommate's new baby. That all seemed innocent enough, didn't it? Just exactly when had she stepped out of the real world and into this wonderland where everything was upside-down?

It was all so strange. There was a break in the wind, and snow was falling in tiny, glittering flakes, falling silently all around, hitting her face with small, frosty impacts and melting there. It had been years since she'd even seen snow, not since her college days in Northern California, when they'd all packed up the car and headed for the mountains to try out the ski lifts. It always made her marvel how the snow could change the landscape in such a short time and never make a sound. It was like magic—as though some wizard had waved a wand and transformed everything when no one was looking. An enchanted episode.

And so was this whole situation. Was this really happening? Was she in the middle of some off-the-wall nightmare?

"If you cannot afford an attorney, one will be appointed for you."

She sighed and began to shiver uncontrollably. No, she wasn't dreaming. It was all crazy, but very real.

"This is a joke, right? You're just trying to scare me." She half turned so that she could see his face again, look into his eyes, search for a spark of humor. "Hey, I promise. No more speeding, honest. I'll be a good girl from now on. In fact, I'll stay away from driving altogether and get myself a chauffeur. How about that?"

He didn't seem to hear her, his eyes as opaque as ever. "Do you have any questions? Have you understood these rights I've just read you?"

She shook her head, feeling silly, and gripped her arms tightly around herself. "I don't understand anything at all."

His mouth twisted and he gestured toward her. "Hold your hands out behind your back."

"What?"

The handcuffs were on before she knew what was happening, and she was so shocked she couldn't utter a word.

"Let's go."

She turned to look at him, aghast. "But why?" she asked weakly, too stunned to fight for the moment. "What have I done?"

"Armed robbery, for starters." He pointed her toward his car, and she went along in a fog of disbelief, his hand guiding her. "That was in Utah. Arizona said something about kidnapping. Colorado mentioned bunco. And then there was the little matter of a shooting in Laughlin, Nevada. Remember that one?"

"No," she said, shaking her head, dazed. "No!" she repeated more loudly. She stopped, eyes blazing as her spirit revived. She was no criminal. There was a mistake being made. He had to listen to reason. It was silly, really, in a perverted sort of way. Surely he would see the joke if she just explained. "No, this is crazy," she told him, shaking her head. "I've never done any of those things. I've never even been to Laughlin."

"Get in the car." He held open a door to the back seat.

She stared in at the interior of the car. It looked grotesquely lonely. He couldn't do this. Could he? She started shaking her head again, backing away. "No, I..."

Reaching out, he gave her an encouraging push that brooked no argument or hesitation. She got in awkwardly, her hands stretched out behind her.

"Okay, wise guy," she muttered, anger beginning to rise in her. "Okay," she said more forcefully, turning to look at him, her cheeks bright with the humiliation. "If you think you know so much about me, tell me this. Who do you think I am?"

He flipped up a clipboard from the front seat and scanned it. "Billie Joe Calloway of Fort Worth, Texas," he read off what he had clipped there. "Twenty-eight years old and good-looking. Five foot six with nice curves. Golden blond hair. Blue eyes. Driving a green Ford Mustang with California plates." He dropped the clipboard and looked at her. "Now, doesn't that sound familiar?" he asked her softly, his eyes as cold as an Arctic winter.

If it wasn't so scary, the situation might have been funny. But right now it would be pretty hard to work up a real, honest laugh out of it.

"I'm thirty," she said quickly. "And I'm not from Texas. Do you hear even one tiny hint of a Texas twang in this voice?" But when you came right down to it, the rest fit her to a tee. "I'm not this Billie Joe person," she said more strongly, glaring at him for emphasis. "You've got the wrong woman this time."

She thought quickly. There had to be some way to prove it. Of all the times to lose her purse. "Oh, my car registration!"

He shrugged. "So you stole a car."

"Oh, I see. No matter what I come up with, you'll have a reason why it doesn't apply." She stared at him in exasperation. "You're going to feel like such an idiot when you find out the truth."

He shrugged again, seeming totally disinterested. "We'll see," he said as he swung into the driver's seat.

"My car," she protested, suddenly realizing they were going to drive off and leave it. "It's just sitting there. Someone will take it."

He turned and looked at her through the opening in the glass partition between the seats. "Don't you get it?" he said, his voice soft but tough. "There is no one around, Miss Calloway. You took the wrong road, all right. You must have gone past three separate barriers to get this far. You were on a street to nowhere when I picked out your headlights and came on out here to see what was going on." He started up his engine. "If you'd gone a mile farther, you'd have probably driven right off a cliff," he added, sounding almost cheerful for once, "since you seem to have an opposite reaction to warning signs, or any other sort of rules or regulations."

Cami turned slowly and looked back, squinting into the blurry white wilderness, dumbfounded. Was he right? She didn't remember any barriers. So now she was supposed to consider him her savior instead of her enemy? It didn't make any sense, but it served to keep her quiet as they rode down the mountain and turned onto a highway. She was thinking things over—and getting more and more puzzled all the time.

"My purse," she murmured hopelessly at one point.

"The snow's getting too deep to find it now," he told her. "I'll send someone out in the morning to look for it."

She lapsed into silence again, overwhelmed by it all. She'd been in scrapes before. In fact, she'd been known by her friends as someone who seemed to attract trouble. She liked to think of it as trouble attracting her. And she usually had no problem in dealing with such things. But nothing in her background and experience had prepared her for this, and it was going to take some time to pull herself together and figure how to get out of this one.

"This is utterly outrageous," she said, staring at his rock-hard profile. "You can't just go around arresting people like this."

"Sure I can," he responded, glancing back at her. "It's my job."

Two

Okay, so this was going to be a little more complicated than he'd thought. Rafe eased the car around the corner, wheels spinning in the snow, and avoided looking in the rearview mirror. With the storm coming in, he was probably going to be stuck with her for the night. Oh, well. It came with the job. And it had been so long since he'd arrested anyone, he'd almost forgotten how to do it.

"Here we are," he said as the car slid to a stop beside the old adobe building. "Hold on a minute. I'll get your door."

He wasn't being gallant, merely careful. With the rap sheet this lady carried in her background, he wasn't going to take any chances. She was tougher than she looked—had to be, with the things she'd done lately. He held the door and watched her emerge awkwardly from the car, and then wished he hadn't.

She had the longest damn legs he'd seen in some time. And what was she doing wearing a skirt up here in the mountains, anyway? Nobody wore skirts around here. And if she had to wear a skirt, why couldn't she control it better? She didn't have to let it hike halfway up like that.

He knew that was hardly fair. After all, she was still in handcuffs. Still, it made him feel better to complain, even silently. The way she moved did allow him to get a good look at some of the most beautiful legs he'd ever gawked at, but that wasn't what he wanted to do—not at her. She was a suspect, for Pete's sake. He wasn't supposed to notice her legs, or anything else about her. It wasn't professional. He swore at himself and looked away. No, this definitely was no cinch.

"We'll go on in," he told her, turning her and pointing her in the right direction. "We'll get the proper forms filled out, and then we'll call Santa Fe." There was still a chance they would come on out and pick her up right away. It all depended on how badly they wanted her.

"Okay," she said absently, gazing about herself.

A city girl all the way, Cami had been expecting a nice brick building swarming with experience-toughened cops who would be crusty but ready to hear the truth if it were presented correctly. One call to some sort of centralized information bank, one check of the picture with the arrest warrant for Billie Joe, one look at Cami herself in the light, and this whole fabrication of her supposed criminal career would crumble into the dust. Apologies all around. Someone would drive her back to her car and send her on her way. And it would be all over.

No such luck.

"This is it?" she asked in wonder as he led her through the thickening snowbanks into the small adobe building set right against the street. She looked to the right and to the left and saw no more than three or four small buildings set back along the side of the road, one of which had a sign that read Country Store and had a bus stop designation hanging out front. The place was barely a crossroads, much less a town.

"This is your police station?" Standing in the middle of the floor, she looked from side to side at the desk, the table and two chairs, the television set, the small, old-fashioned cell in the corner of the room. "Where's the rest of it?"

The only sign that he'd heard her was a slight twitch at the corner of his mouth as he came in behind her, shrugging out of his jacket. With one quick, deft movement, he unlocked the handcuffs and removed them, setting them down on the desk beside the hat he had just removed, as well, then pulled up a chair. "Sit down and we'll get the paperwork started," he suggested.

"This looks like something right out of an old Western movie," she said, still looking around nervously and rubbing her wrists. "A relic."

"It is," he told her calmly, dropping into the desk chair and pulling a typewriter into position. "It's been here since 1889."

"That's over a hundred years." She tucked her arms in close and shivered, as though the ghosts of all that history were treading on her space.

"You got it."

Looking down, she eyed the ancient machine he was adjusting. "Is that why you still use a typewriter? Just to keep in line with the historical accuracy of the place?" She pointed to the television in the corner of the room. "In which case, that's certainly an anachronism you ought to get rid of."

He gestured toward the chair once more and said with cool formality, "I still use a typewriter because the good people of this little town can't afford to buy me a computer."

She sat down with a thump and glared at him, annoyed that he was ordering her around, even if silently, and even more annoyed with herself for letting him get away with it. "I guess that means they probably got you dirt cheap, too, doesn't it?"

He looked her full in the face and his voice hardened. "It does. But no matter what I get paid, I'm still the sheriff. That means I'm the law here, lady." It was something he was going to have to remember around this woman. "I think it's time you stopped and thought that over."

She did, but only for a moment. She resented his tone, and she told him so.

He gave her a long-suffering look. "Okay, if you want to argue about every detail of this arrest, we can do that. But that will only delay filling out the forms I need before I call Santa Fe and get to the bottom of this."

She knew he was right, but she could hardly help complaining. After all, this was a case of mistaken identity. How dare he keep her here this way? "Meanwhile I get to cool my heels here in a jail cell?" she said, looking over her shoulder at the bars and shuddering lightly.

His gaze darkened as he looked at her. Her hair was floating around her face in a cloud of silver and gold that set off the crystal blue of her eyes. He'd noticed the shudder and he assumed it was part of her act. He had to admit, she was damn good. "Look at it this way—it'll keep you out of trouble for an hour or so."

Her chin rose and she glared at him. "I don't need to be kept out of trouble."

He shrugged, turning away. "It's pretty obvious you need a keeper of some kind," he muttered.

"Hey, I don't like the sound of that." He didn't seem to care, so she got tougher. "What are you, some kind of sexist pig?" she said pointedly.

That got his attention. He turned back and stared at her, his eyes hard as tinted glass. "Excuse me?" he said icily.

She turned down the corners of her mouth and lifted her chin. "That was a purely sexist comment."

He considered her words for a moment, tilting his head to the side, before shaking it slowly. "No, I don't think so," he drawled at last. "I would have said the same to any criminal, male or female."

She flushed, but luckily he'd already turned away again, so he didn't see it.

"You're the one who's going to look ridiculous when it all comes out and you see that I was absolutely right," she told him quickly. "I am Cami Bishop. I've never even heard of this Billie Joe person." He didn't respond, and she tried again. "Who am I going to have to see to get compensated for this outrage? I'm going to sue the pants off you and your town."

"You can certainly try," he said casually, taking papers and pens out of his drawer and setting up for the paperwork. "It's within your rights." Looking up, he met her gaze. "But that would mean you'd have to come back and hang around here for weeks, maybe months."

She made a face. "You're right. It wouldn't be worth it."

For the first time, she really took a look at the man who was causing her so much trouble. His dark hair was thick and worn a little too long in back and lightly touched with silver at the temples, as though a few snowflakes still clung to him from the storm outside. There was a primitive strength to him. His face was handsome in a hard, emotionless way, dark, all granite planes and angles, with deep grooves that almost made him look bitter. Something about him fit the place, though. He might have been here in 1889, back in cowboy-and-Indian days. And she wouldn't know which category to place him in. With his dark skin and wind-weathered look, he could have fit in either one.

Sheriff Rafe Lonewolf was what the sign on his desk called him. She could see traces of Native American ancestry in his face, but other things were mixed in with it. He looked tough, as though he were used to using his fists as well as his brain to get himself out of trouble. She searched his expression, but there was no humor, no empathy. Was this just the mask he put on to do his job, she wondered? Or was this the real thing?

"If I do decide to file, I guess you're the one I'll have to name in my unlawful arrest lawsuit, huh?" she said brightly, wondering if she could get a rise out of him and not stopping to realize that might not be such a good idea. "I hope your little town can afford that judgment."

She watched him for a moment, but there was no response, no change in his expression. So what now? Should she say something more impertinent, try to get his goat? Probably not. But how was she going to get out of this? A gust of wind rattled the windows and she pulled her chair up a little closer, glad that at least she was out of the storm.

But that wasn't going to be enough to satisfy her for long. "When do I get my phone call?" she asked, looking around the room restlessly.

He glanced at her, then looked away. "As soon as we get this paperwork out of the way."

"I think I'll use my call to order a pizza," she quipped, leaning back as though she were sure of herself. "By the time we get the paperwork done, you'll realize you made a big mistake and I'll be ready to get on my way. A nice hot pizza would hit the spot about then." She smiled. *So there,* her expression said, even if her mouth didn't actually form the words.

He looked at her balefully as he rolled a form into the typewriter. How had he gotten so lucky, anyway? It had been a nice quiet night. In fact, it had been a nice, quiet life since he'd taken this job out here in the sticks. He liked it that way. He'd had enough of the rough stuff down in the city to last him a lifetime. Peace and quiet were slowly healing a lot of wounds he'd collected down there.

But something told him it couldn't last. Not now that Billie Joe Calloway had hit town and entered his jurisdiction.

He had no doubt that he had the right person in custody. After all, how many beautiful blondes in green Mustangs would be cruising through Clear Creek during any given space of time? Not many. This area was so out-of-the-way, they didn't even have a real gas station—just the pump at Gray Eagle's farm. Not too many tourists cruised through here. That was why he'd barely paid any attention to the bulletin that Billie Joe might be in the area when it had first come in that morning.

No, the idea that two blondes in identical cars might drive through stretched credulity a bit past the breaking point. And the prospect of having two of them in one weekend would be more than he could handle, he thought with a surge of humor he was careful not to show to her.

He glanced at her, letting himself look her over for a moment. He had to admit she didn't look much like the usual criminals he'd dealt with in the past. There was a softness to her they usually didn't show. Her expensive clothes and jewelry didn't impress him. He'd arrested women before who'd looked like they belonged in Beverly Hills. But there was something about those blue eyes. They flashed with annoyance, but not with craft. And the rest of her—he only allowed himself one quick, cursory look and his immediate response served to warn him not to do that again. Her body was as pretty as her face, curves that nicely strained the fabric of her clothes and sent a rush up his thermometer. That wasn't supposed to happen. He couldn't let her get to him. He looked away, hardening his face even more, determined not to let her know she was in any way attractive in the cold eyes of the law.

He typed in a few spaces, then sighed softly and sat back. "Name?" he asked, though he knew it was probably going to lead to another argument. The night stretched out long and unpleasant before him.

"Cami Bishop," she said smartly. "Cambria Shasta Bishop, if you want to get formal about it." She added her date and place of birth. "Unmarried."

He nodded, typing in the information she was giving, though he knew he was going to have to fill out another form with what he assumed was the more accurate version. The warrant said, though she was currently unmarried, she'd been married three times. He glanced at her from under lowered brows, wondering about such a young woman with three marriages behind her, but he couldn't see any evidence of her past on her face. In fact, she looked far too open and trusting to be the sort of man-eating babe the warrant portrayed. But looks were deceiving. He'd learned that lesson before.

"Occupation?"

She hesitated. For some reason, it was always hard to explain that one to people. "I publish a fern journal," she said at last.

His mouth twisted with obvious annoyance. "You mean a foreign journal?" he asked, looking at her.

She shook her head and held back a sudden urge to giggle. "No. I told you I wasn't from Texas, didn't I? The word is *fern*. You know, those green plants that grow in shady forests."

"Oh. Botany." He glanced at her linen suit and soft leather shoes and frowned skeptically. "You don't look much like a nature freak," he noted coolly.

"Oh, I'm not," she assured him quickly, amused by the thought herself. "I don't actually go out and tromp in the woods or anything like that."

He looked slightly pained. "Of course not."

She heard the sarcasm but chose to ignore it. "No, I edit research articles scientists submit."

She was something all right. She said these things with a cool patina of honesty that could almost fool you. He had to hold back the grin that wanted to steal into his expression. "I see. You don't get your hands dirty."

She smiled as though she could sense his amusement. "Only with printer's ink."

He abandoned the typewriter and faced her, his natural skepticism plain to see. This was just too much. "Who the hell reads something like that?" If she could answer that one, he'd have to hand it to her. She could manufacture the whoppers.

She gazed back in wide-eyed innocence, her answer ready. "Other scientists. Hobbyists. People who like ferns."

Throwing his head back, he groaned, "Right."

For the first time, she thought she detected the barest glint of amusement in his eyes, but this time it didn't make her smile. "You think I'm making this all up, don't you?" she cried with sudden insight.

He stared into her eyes for a moment, then nodded and shrugged. "Of course you are."

She shook her head in wonder. It was finally sinking in. He really thought she was the outlaw. This wasn't just some strange coincidence. She was being booked. She might go to jail. Impossible as that was to believe, it seemed to be coming true. A small flare of panic lit in her breast. She had to do something.

"Where's the warrant?" she asked, leaning forward and pressing her lips together with new determination.

"The warrant?" His dark gaze was veiled.

"For this Billie Joe Calloway's arrest." She put out her hand authoritatively. "Let me see it. I want to see the picture."

He hesitated, gazing at her speculatively. "There is no picture."

"What?"

"I don't have a fax. We're out in the country here, in case you hadn't noticed. I have to wait for mail. I just got the information on you today, mixed in with a long list of fugitives from the law." He glanced at a stack of papers on his desk. "I will tell you this. You're listed as one of the three most dangerous."

She groaned and looked at him beseechingly. "But it's not me! Don't you get it? I'm innocent."

He turned away. There was no point in getting into a hassle over this. "Hey, tell it to the judge," he murmured, rolling the paper into a new position in his typewriter.

"I'd love to," she snapped, tossing her thick blond hair. "Where is he? When do I get to see him?"

He squinted at the window, plastered white with wind-driven snow. "I don't know. With this storm, it may be a while. Considering the judge is in Santa Fe."

"Santa Fe?" She'd been there only that afternoon. It seemed like days ago. Another lifetime. "That's almost three hours away."

"You got that right." He nodded, eyeing her. "Three hours on a sunny day."

She stared at him in horror. It had all seemed so simple at first. Now she was beginning to get the picture, and the scene before her was abhorrent.

"So, even though I'm innocent, I have to sit around here for hours and hours, waiting to prove it?"

He didn't look up. There seemed to be an awful lot of words and numbers he had to fill into slots on the form. "Looks like," he murmured, his voice barely audible, as though she hardly counted any longer.

He was a very annoying man and she was beginning to get really angry. This was all his fault. Anyone with any sense would have realized long ago that she wasn't a criminal. She glared at him furiously, but he didn't look up, so the effect was lost.

"Well, there has to be somewhere we can call, something we can do." Cami wasn't used to being told there was nothing she could do. She was used to action, to coming across a problem and dealing with it right then and there. She moved restlessly in her chair, anxious to get on it. "I suppose a lawyer would be hours away in Santa Fe, as well?"

He nodded. "I'm not asking you to make a statement until we get hold of one."

"How very thoughtful of you," she noted dryly. But hardly helpful. There had to be another way to attack this thing. "Where did you get the listing from, anyway? Maybe we could call them. Or we could call the different police who claim Billie Joe did these things. Just ask them a few questions and I'm sure you'll start to see she's not me. Or I'm not her. Or whatever."

He nodded again. He was planning to do those very things, but not until he had the paperwork done. Forms were the worst part of the job, but they had to be filled out. "We'll make some calls. All in good time."

He went back to his work and she swung her feet, impatient and frustrated. Her mind went back over the past few weeks—how she'd received the invitation from her best friend from college, Sara Parker, to come to her baby shower in Denver—how she'd planned her trip with stops along the way to visit with some of her regular contributors to the journal—how they'd wined and dined her in Santa Fe and sent her on her way much later than she'd planned—and how the storm had caught up with her. And now she was here, sitting in this ancient building with this disturbing man, accused of being Billie Joe Calloway. It was all so ridiculous.

She glanced at the sheriff. He was going to feel awfully foolish when the truth came out. Right now, that was her only solace. She could tell he was a proud man, used to being right. It wasn't going to be easy for him to face this mistake.

Good. Served him right.

"Do you have any tea?" she asked, looking around. "A nice cup of tea would taste so good right now."

He shook his head, not looking up. "There's a coffeepot by the TV," he said. "Go ahead and pour yourself a cup."

"Coffee?" She shuddered. "No thanks, that would just make me shaky. I only drink coffee for breakfast. You're sure you don't have a little tea bag hiding around here somewhere?"

"No." He glanced at her coolly, his gaze just skimming her, not lingering too long in any one place. "No tea. Just coffee. Take it or leave it."

She stared at him, affronted by his attitude, but at the same time, she knew she was being ridiculous. He wasn't her host, after all. He'd arrested her. He couldn't be expected to provide hospitality, now could he? Still, she couldn't help but resent it.

"No tea," she muttered. "No fax machine. How do you get fingerprints and stuff like that? Do you have to wait for the mail for that, too?" She paled, suddenly realizing just exactly what that meant, and when she spoke again, her voice was pitched higher. "Am I going to have to wait for the mail in order to get out of here?"

He glanced at her, then back down at his paper. "Don't worry," he told her smoothly. "Either Santa Fe will send someone for you, or I'll take you down in the morning."

No. Something had to give before that. Morning seemed very far away right now. Rising, she paced restlessly through the room. She had to get out of here. There was just no way she was staying. Somehow, something had to be done. But what? The storm was slashing snow against the windows and whistling through the tiles on the roof. It was dangerous out there. She whirled, feeling frustrated.

"Previous arrest record?" he asked, and she spun, dropping back down to sit in the chair.

"None," she said crisply. "Unless you count the time old Mr. Campbell caught me stealing gum out of the broken gum machine at his store when I was ten years old."

He looked up at her. He couldn't help it. He looked up at her and he noted her eyes, the pale blue of icy Arctic caverns, and her pretty mouth—it looked soft and smooth and very warm. Fire and ice—an intriguing combination, a pairing that stirred him in ways he didn't want to admit.

And then he looked away and uttered a few obscenities silently and to himself. He had to keep from doing things like that. If he didn't watch out, he would let her see the way she was affecting him, and if that happened, he would have a hard time maintaining his authority over her. He knew very well what could happen, the games men and women played with one another. And he wasn't going to let himself get pulled into them.

"What did he do to you?" he asked gruffly, forcing his mind back to the childhood story she was telling.

She thought back, her eyes suddenly dreamy. "He gave me a lecture and made me sweep the floor." An irrepressible smile curled her lips at the memories. "And then he gave me a whole bag of gum balls to take home. I was the most popular kid on the street that night."

"Ah." He nodded wisely, a sardonic look in his eyes. "So that's what started you on your road to crime. You found you could gain popularity from handing out things that didn't belong to you to your friends."

Her jaw dropped and she sputtered incoherently. Grinning, he pulled out the paper and turned it to fill in the back, feeling very pleased with himself for having annoyed her. "Education?" he asked.

"Hidden Valley College in Marin County." She looked at him defiantly. "I graduated, too."

"Congratulations." He typed in the words. "Well-educated criminals are the best kind."

"Oh!" Exasperated, she rose again, throwing a quick glare his way, and went back to pacing the room. "If you weren't a cop..."

She left the threat up in the air, but it hit home. He was a cop and he'd better not forget it. Looking at her, he wished he could take her back up on the ridge route and start this all over again. Somehow they had gotten off on the wrong foot. He wasn't acting like himself at all. He was usually cool and detached, a complete professional. Where had he lost that reserve? To make up for it, he was going to have to be tougher than usual. Mean. Could he be mean to her?

She turned her head and her golden curls danced in the harsh light and something curled inside him like a coiled spring. He groaned silently. No, he couldn't be mean to her. And if he didn't watch out, the cop in him would disappear, and the man was going to take over. No matter what, he couldn't let that happen. Hardening his mouth, he tried to harden his heart at the same time, and years of practice made it that much easier to do.

"Let's just get this done, Miss Calloway," he said firmly.

She glanced at him and frowned, wanting to shake him, wanting to shake up everything and get to the truth. The truth should be plain for him to see, if he would only look at her without all his preconceived ideas.

"This is crazy," she muttered, still pacing. Suddenly she found herself nearing the corner of the room she'd been avoiding, where the bars were, and her steps slowed. Reaching out, she tentatively touched the lock on the little cell. The door swung away from her and she stared into a space hardly big enough to keep a cat in. There was a simple cot and a chair, and that was it. Was she going to end up spending the night in that place? No way!

She turned back to look at the sheriff, scared but unwilling to let him see it. "You call this a jail?" she said scornfully.

He barely looked up, still involved in paperwork. "It's got bars, doesn't it?"

She made a face at him, secure in the knowledge that he couldn't see it. "So does the Las Vegas strip."

He nodded, then looked up and actually cracked what might be considered a smile. ''Yeah, but I don't have the key to that,'' he said.

Their gazes met, the lights flickered as a gust of wind hit the building, and something else happened.

She wasn't sure what it was, but it hit her hard. Time seemed to stand still. His dark eyes turned smoky with a mystery she suddenly felt an aching need to unravel. All in a moment, she was intimately aware of his wide, sensuous mouth, his rock-hard shoulders, his long, lean, muscular hands. At the same time, she was alive to an acceptance within herself of an emotional embrace. This was not at all like her, and scared her to death. She'd never felt anything like this.

''No,'' she whispered, still staring into his eyes. ''No.'' And then, finally, she tore her gaze away from his. ''No, I'm out of here,'' she muttered, rejecting it all as she whirled and began a headlong flight for the door.

He swore softly as he sprang up to catch her. ''What the hell do you think you're doing?'' he demanded, grabbing her by the arm and jerking her around to face him.

She stared up at him as though she were afraid of what she might see, and shook her head. If he hadn't sensed what she'd sensed, so much the better. But it didn't really help her. ''I can't stay here with you,'' she said hoarsely.

His head went back and his eyes took on a distant look. ''Why not?''

But she couldn't put it into words. Putting it into words would mean acknowledging it, and that would only make things worse.

It seemed he hadn't felt the stinging connection she thought she'd experienced. That was a relief, she supposed. Maybe. Or maybe he was just pretending not to notice. Or maybe he made these sensual links with women all the time.

Well, she didn't. And she wasn't about to go where such things inevitably led. What she really had to do was get out of here.

"I...I just can't, that's all. Let me go. Come on." She looked up at him beseechingly. "You know, deep down, that I'm not a criminal. Just let me go and I won't tell anyone you ever saw me. Nobody will know and..."

"Stop it," he demanded, frowning at her as his fingers tightened on her arm. "Don't get all worked up. There's no point to it." He jerked his head toward the outside world. "You hear that wind? You can't go out in this storm, no matter how innocent you are. You're stuck here. You might as well relax."

Relax? Relax? When every nerve ending was quivering inside her? She took a long, deep breath and closed her eyes.

He was right. She couldn't go anywhere until morning. At least she wasn't huddled in her car on the side of the road, wondering if she was going to freeze to death.

She opened her eyes again and managed a bleak smile. "Okay," she said softly, pulling away from his touch and turning back into the room. "I guess I'm more tired than I realized."

But her gaze flickered from one corner of the room to another, looking for a possible escape route, something he noted with a cynical gleam in his eyes. He took hold of her again, by the shoulders this time, just to drive the point home. "Don't get any more ideas, lady," he said firmly. "You're not leaving here until I let you go."

She stood stock-still, her gaze icy. It was obvious to her that she was going to have to defend herself against him—or at least, against letting him beguile her in any way. "You're touching me," she said. "That's not allowed, is it?"

His fingers tightened, and so did his mouth. She was getting to him at last. Anger was smoldering in his dark eyes.

"Isn't it?" he said softly. "It all depends on whose rules we're following." But he released her, standing back as she flexed her shoulders and glared at him.

"You'd better just hope I don't get any bruises," she said smartly. "I'll charge you with police brutality."

His head went back. "You know all the buzzwords, don't you?" Real anger shot through him like a hot gulp of whiskey.

Those were city words, words he hadn't heard for a long time, words he had come here to forget. Around here, he was a part of the community. Everybody knew him. Everybody turned to him with their problems, with their worries, anytime they needed help—not every time they needed a scapegoat. No one here would ever think to charge him with brutality. It made him angry to have her bring city words and city concepts here. He reached out and took up the handcuffs, then turned toward her with a glint in his eyes.

"Tell you what," he said, eyes narrowing. "I'm going to have to put the cuffs back on you."

She shrank back. "No!"

He moved toward her, holding the cuffs up where she could see them. "You tried to make a break for it, lady. You're not cooperating like you should. There's no reason not to suspect you might do it again. You don't have a leg to stand on."

She glared at him, but when she spoke, she worked hard to keep her voice low and polite. "I'm sorry I did that," she said, backing away as she spoke. "I won't do it again. Honest."

He watched her for a moment, dangling the cuffs before her. "It's your choice," he told her at last. "As long as I can trust you..."

"Oh, you can trust me," she assured him hurriedly. "Believe me, you can trust me."

He hesitated. She was saying the right words, but the look in her eyes told him she was feeling anything but meek. Still, what was he going to do, tie her up?

No, he reminded himself. He was going to put her in a cell.

And even at that, a part of him cringed. She was so pretty, so...

No. He turned and dropped the handcuffs on the desk. What was the matter with him? He'd locked up prettier women than this, back in Los Angeles. There was that time he'd been in on that raid of the porno movie set in Burbank. And the time he and his partner had broken a ring of young women who pretended to sell cosmetics door-to-door but were really casing the houses for visits later on in the night. And Doris, the sticky-fingered contortionist. Gorgeous women, every one. He'd locked them up without a qualm. And he was going to do the same here.

But not yet. They still had paperwork to finish. It could wait.

Three

Rafe Lonewolf, sheriff, and Billie Joe Calloway, con artist extraordinaire. This was going to be some night. He looked at her narrowly, and she looked right back. It was evident that whatever had spooked her a few minutes earlier was under control now. She had her confidence back, and her spirit.

She plunked herself in the chair and he sat back down in front of the typewriter, and she watched for a moment as he filled in spaces on the form.

He was just a man. And as the song went, she'd known a lot of men before. Now that her pulse had calmed and her nerves had steadied, she couldn't imagine what had upset her so much a few minutes earlier. She couldn't let this situation, this man, this night, get to her. She was woman, she was strong, and all that. And he was just a man.

And she was no victim. She could hold her own, and she could act like an equal. She could, in fact, go on the offense. That was often the best defensive strategy anyway.

Put him off his guard. Keep him guessing. She wet her lips and launched her game plan.

"That's quite a little Hitler complex you've got there," she said, speaking softly, as though she were musing about an interesting detail rather than accusing him of being a world-class despot.

He glanced up, determined not to take her too seriously. "No. I've got a cop complex. That's all."

"Hmm," she reflected, studying her fingernails. "Suspicious, cynical, mean. It can't be much fun going through life like that."

He leaned back in his chair and looked at her as though she'd brought up speaking ancient Greek as a recreational activity. "Fun isn't what life is all about," he reminded her.

She nodded. "You're right. But it sure does help you get over the rough spots." She glanced around the room. "What do you do around here for fun? Or is arresting innocent people the way you get your kicks?"

"No. I work. I sleep. I read."

She stared at him. Suddenly she was really concerned. "That's it?" she said incredulously. So that was the answer, that was what made him so mean. He was a grouch because he was badly socialized. Hope surged again. Cami was a can-do woman, and she liked nothing better than finding potential solutions to problems. She'd been struggling with this problem, this man, for about an hour now. And finally she saw light at the end of the tunnel.

Nothing could be simpler. All she had to do was make friends with him, like you would a snarling dog, bit by bit, offering a snack, extending a hand...

"Listen, you need to break out of your routine," she told him kindly. "You need something new in your life."

"Thanks, but no thanks."

He didn't look grateful for her sensitive suggestions. Still, these things took time.

He typed another line in the form and she frowned, trying to think of something to offer him. "You know, I'm
probably a faster typist than you are," she said. "Would
you like me to fill it out?"

She could have sworn he was rolling his eyes, but he didn't
turn back to face her, so she couldn't tell for sure.

"No," he said simply.

"Could I get you a fresh cup of coffee?"

"No, thanks."

Her mouth tightened. If he wasn't going to cooperate, this
experiment in the building of an understanding between
them was going to be harder than she'd thought at first. A
tiny doubt tugged at her. What if he were incapable of un-
bending? What if he were just born mean, and that was
that? But she couldn't accept anything so hopeless. She was
made of sterner stuff. She pressed on, thinking hard.

Suddenly she sat up straighter, struck with an idea. "How
about this? How long has it been since you've had your
fortune read?"

That got to him. He turned and stared at her. "My
what?"

She stuck out her slim fingers. "Give me your hand," she
ordered.

"What?"

"Your hand," she said impatiently. "Let me see it."

He shook his head. No way. Was she crazy? The prisoner did not act like this. Prisoners were scared and hesi-
tant, or they were brash and unruly, in which case they had
to be cuffed. One or the other. Prisoners did not offer to
make you cups of coffee. Prisoners did not ask to see your
hand.

So why was it that he was extending that very same hand,
palm up, and letting her hold it? He didn't know. Forces
beyond his understanding seemed to be at work here. They
weren't following the rules. Things were very close to spinning out of control.

Her touch was cool and smooth and light. He felt a strange buzzing in his ears as she held his hand, like the fleeting high from a quick drink taken on an empty stomach. He was crazy to let this go on. But it sure did feel nice.

His hand was in hers and she was studying it closely, noting its clean, hard lines, its strength. He had nice hands with straight nails and hard yet uncallused palms. She liked them. But she wasn't going to let things go in that direction again, so she sealed off that side of her emotions and got on with it.

"You've got a long life line," she told him, gazing down thoughtfully. "Look." She traced it with her finger. "Look how far it goes. I've never seen one this long before."

"And you probably never will again," he noted dryly. "That's an old scar from breaking up a bar fight." His mouth quirked at the corners. "I didn't know at the time it would add years to my life, or I would have done it more often."

"Oh." Her gaze met his and they almost laughed together.

Almost, but not quite. They caught themselves in time. Rafe pulled back his hand.

"Some fortune-teller. You'd better keep your day job," he advised her.

"Wait," she protested quickly. "I haven't got to the part about the tall, dark stranger in your future yet."

His mouth twisted in a way that might have been a smile, but she wasn't really sure. "I think a short, ditzy blonde in my present is more like it," he said gruffly, turning back to the desk. "We've got to finish this paperwork if you ever want to get to the call to Santa Fe."

She made a face at him, knowing he wouldn't see it. "I'm not short," she said softly, but he ignored it.

She sighed. So it did no good to get friendly with him. Back to square one, and the original plan. When in doubt, tough it out. That was what her father always used to tell her. Funny but she'd never realized his words to live by would come in handy someday. She had to curb her natural inclination to be reasonable and give everyone the benefit of the doubt. She knew what her rights were. Maybe it was about time to see that they were upheld by this country sheriff.

"When do I get to make my phone call?" she demanded, prepared to fight about it.

"When I'm good and ready to let you make it."

"I have rights," she reminded him, raising one eyebrow. "Does it usually take this long? Or am I just special?"

He met her gaze and held it, as though evaluating his options. Finally he picked up the phone and plunked it down in front of her. "Go ahead. Just keep it short." But as she picked up the receiver and began to dial, he reached out to stop her, adding, "Who are you calling?"

She held the receiver away from him and frowned at him furiously, sure he was still trying to thwart her. "Do I have to tell you? Is that in the rules?"

He looked pained. "I'm not trying to figure out your strategy. I just wanted to advise you to be careful who you call and how you do it. By law, you get one call. Once it's gone, it's gone."

She frowned suspiciously, not ready to accept that at face value. "But if the first phone call doesn't work out, surely there's another one allowed."

Squaring his shoulders, he couldn't keep the gleam of satisfaction out of his voice. "Nope."

Her eyes sparked. "The deck is really stacked in your favor, isn't it?"

"Of course," he said simply. Then he almost grinned. "I'm the good guy."

"In your dreams." She shook her head, exasperated. He was enjoying this a little too much. Sadistic beast. She turned away so that her back was to him and began to dial again. But something wasn't right. Holding the receiver to her ear, she frowned. "There's no dial tone," she said, turning back to him. "Listen." She held it out to him.

He listened, then tapped down the buttons a few times and gave up. "It's dead," he said shortly.

She stared at him, hoping he didn't mean what he obviously did mean. This telephone was her only hope, her only lifeline to the outside world that would surely prove, quickly enough once contacted, that she wasn't any more Billie Joe Calloway than she was Billy the Kid. "Dead? What do you mean, it's dead?"

He glanced at her, his eyes as dark as coal. He knew what she was thinking, and he knew more than that. This meant the die was cast. The two of them were going to spend the night together in this room. There was no longer any way out. "It's dead. The storm's probably knocked out the lines."

The look of horror on her face mirrored her distress. She was feeling more and more isolated here, more and more helpless. Was there no escape from this situation? "But... what about my phone call?"

He raised that dark eyebrow again, and the look on his face was a cynical one. "Got a cellular phone?"

Her eyes lit up. "Back in my car."

He gestured toward the snowstorm raging outside the window. "Then I guess you're out of luck."

"But that's not fair!"

He wasn't sure why, but he was feeling rather smug at the moment. "No. Neither are lotteries or beauty pageants, but we have them anyway."

She shook her head. "There's got to be something." A note of desperation was edging her tone.

He turned from her and gestured toward a dark, old-fashioned-looking machine sitting against the back of the desk. "There's the old shortwave," he told her reluctantly. "It's ancient and it doesn't work very well. But at least I might be able to get through to the district office in Santa Fe."

"Okay." She spread her arms out. "Let's do it."

She sat down and watched as he fooled with the controls for what seemed like hours, and finally there was a crackling sound of someone on the line.

"Hey, Jasper. That you?" Rafe shouted into the microphone.

"Yeah, it's me," a thin, reedy voice answered. "Hey, Rafe. What's up?"

"I'm trying to get through to Santa Fe or Albuquerque."

There was more crackling, then the voice again. "Give it up, man. Can't be done right now. They've got a state of emergency because of this storm, plus there's a fifty-car pileup on the interstate. They've got their hands full tonight. Whatever you got had better wait until morning."

"Oh, brother." She said the words, shaking her head, but somehow this didn't surprise her much. In fact, she'd pretty much been expecting it. When he turned and looked at her, she shrugged her resignation, feeling helpless.

He watched her for a moment, then added, "Even if I get hold of them, they're not going to send anyone up here to get you until tomorrow."

She nodded, beginning to realize she was going to have to accept the inevitable, but still rebellious. She rose again, hugging herself tightly to hold in the despair. "But how am I going to prove my innocence, if we can't even contact the outside world?" she wailed softly.

"You're not." He almost told her he was sorry, but he caught himself in time. "Meanwhile, we'd best get on with things." Pushing away the typewriter, he straightened a stack of paper and prepared to get up, but before he rose, the lights flickered again, and this time they went out.

"Damn," he swore.

"I don't believe this," she murmured, grabbing hold of a nearby chair and dropping into it. "This can't be happening."

He was moving around, opening a cabinet with a metal clang and pulling something out into the room, but she couldn't make out exactly what he was doing. And then a pale splash of light wavered into being, revealing a whole new landscape filled with shadows that hadn't been there before.

"Kerosene lantern," he explained briefly. "No problem. We've got enough fuel to last the night."

She nodded silently, but she wasn't feeling all that relieved. What else could go wrong?

He turned and looked at her, hesitating, then took a deep breath and forced himself to get on with it. "Okay. It's time to get you ready to go into the cell."

The words fell like lead on her spirit. She looked up at him, apprehensive. There was doom gathering at her shoulder and a rain cloud getting ready to unload on her head. Didn't anything ever get better around here? Was it all going to be downhill? "What do you mean, get ready?" she asked warily.

He cleared his throat and turned, to avoid looking her in the eyes. "Regulations require I give you a body search."

He should have done it when they'd first arrived, and he knew it. That had just been one of the many missteps he'd made along the way. Anyone else, and he would have done it immediately.

He'd given her a quick pat-down up at the car, but that wasn't good enough. If she really were Billie Joe—oh hell, now she had him doing it, too. But if she were the suspect, a woman who would trounce hardened criminals at their own game and shoot up a bar in Laughlin, Nevada, she would also be the sort of woman who might very likely have some strange things hidden here and there about her body, just in case. The fact that she hadn't pulled anything on him yet didn't mean a thing. She might be biding her time. He was going to have to take a look.

He hadn't looked at her yet to see her reaction, but he knew she wasn't going to make it easy. He'd heard the sound she'd made when he'd first said it—something between a gasp and a moan. And she hadn't said a word since.

He turned back to look at her. She'd risen from the chair and was standing still as a statue, staring at him hard, and very slowly, very deliberately, shaking her head. Her eyes were huge with the tragedy of her situation, but at the same time, filled with challenge and resolve. She looked very much like a child who was refusing to eat her peas, who, in fact, would die first. And yet he knew she was much more than that. There was steel in that spine. She was no pushover.

"I have to do it," he told her again, hooking his thumbs into the pockets of his slacks and lowering his head, trying to look tough and feeling like an ogre.

She shook her head more vigorously and began to back away. "No," she said hoarsely. "I've put up with a lot of things, mister, but not this. I can't let you do this."

"Regulations," he said curtly, taking a step in her direction.

"To hell with your regulations," she cried. She spun away and put more distance between them. "What would you be looking for?"

He shrugged, taking another step. "Weapons."

"Weapons!" She threw out her hands. "If I had any weapons with me, they would be in my purse, wouldn't they? Do you see any guns strapped to my hips? Any knives in my teeth? I'm not armed, honest. Take my word for it."

"I can't do that."

"But I'm not Billie Joe. Honest. You've got to believe me. I don't need to be searched."

"It's for your own protection," he said, still moving toward her.

"I see." She moved to the side, evading him, and grabbed hold of a file cabinet as though she could use it as a shield. "You wouldn't want me to hang myself with my shoelaces during the night. Is that it?"

"Something like that."

"Don't worry. I'm not suicidal." She backed away, slipping behind another file cabinet and then abandoning that position, as well. "Not yet, anyway," she added, muttering under her breath as she slowly circled the room, back to the wall. "Say," she said, a sudden thought occurring to her. She stopped and straightened to face him. "Don't I get a female warden or something?"

He stopped, too, shaking his head. "Sorry. There's only me."

"Only you." Yeah, and he was the worst one for the job. She couldn't even imagine letting him touch her in the intimate way it would have to be. She had a flashing memory of the way their eyes had met, the way she'd felt for just a moment, and she knew it couldn't happen. She would fight this with every last fiber of her being. Tooth and nail, so to speak. Whatever it took. Facing him, she let him see the determination in her face, the fierce defense she was prepared to muster.

He hesitated, knowing his original thought to strong-arm her wasn't a very good idea. He was a cop, but he wasn't an idiot. There were other ways of doing things, ways that didn't turn everything into an armed confrontation. He was going to have to talk her into this thing. Just how, he wasn't sure. But somehow she was going to have to face reality.

"This is a very small town," he explained, eyeing her narrowly. "There is no female warden. We don't have all the fancy extras for our criminals like you get in the big city."

"I'm not a criminal," she reminded him, just to mark time.

He shrugged, his dark gaze flickering over her. "That remains to be seen. For now, I'll just call you the alleged perpetrator if you prefer."

"Perpetrator?" She nearly laughed aloud. She was definitely in a bad dream and everything sounded like make-believe, Alice-in-Wonderland stuff, but the word *perpetrator* took the cake.

"That's what we used to call you people in the big city."

"Ah, so you've been to civilization before." Keep him talking, she told herself semihysterically. Anything, anything at all to keep him from touching her.

He nodded, though his eyes looked veiled, as though he really didn't want to talk about it. "I've been. I'm back."

"Oh? You didn't like it?"

He winced, thrusting away the memories that topic brought up. "My likes and dislikes aren't relevant," he noted calmly. "We've got a task to perform here. What we have to settle is how we're going to accomplish it."

A glimmer of hope sprang in her chest. That was it—negotiations. She'd give a little, he'd give a little. They'd compromise. Her heart rate started the descent back to normal. Maybe there was a way out after all.

"That's a good idea," she said breathlessly. "Great. Tell you what. You tell me what part you want searched, and I'll do it. I'll give you a running account of what I find and..." She bit her lip in frustration. He was shaking his head. Why was he so obstinate? And it was such a good idea.

"Sorry. Can't be done that way."

"Why not? You can't seriously think I've got things hidden under my clothes."

"You might. I've had it happen before. I once arrested a woman who had a knife hidden in her underpants."

Cami gaped at him. "Do I look like the kind of person who would have a knife in her underwear?"

"You?" He grunted. "You're one of the worst kind. It's always the ones who don't look the part who catch you off guard."

She could see that she was going to have to convince him. "Okay, look here." She slipped out of the linen jacket to her suit and held it out for him to see. "Nothing at all. See?" Tossing it to him so that he could check the lining, she lifted her arms and turned slowly. "No strange bulges, no hidden compartments." She kicked off her shoes and stood before him in her stocking feet. "You see? No razor blades in the shoes. No handguns in the armpits." She looked at him hopefully. Wasn't this enough?

For one brief, flashing second, he thought maybe he was going insane. He'd never done this before, let a woman he'd arrested get to him this way. But standing here, watching her whirl before him, watching her hair sweep out and leave perfume in the air, watching her silk blouse cling to her body, his mouth went dry and his heart began to pound in his chest.

He had to fight it. But he knew one thing—he couldn't touch her. She would be soft to touch, her flesh warm and smooth, and he knew, as though it were something he'd always known, that he wouldn't be able to resist her—that his hands wouldn't stay hard and impersonal, that they would slide down her curves and find places to touch that would leave them both spinning. He made two fists of those hands right now, his knuckles white with the effort, and he worked very hard to keep the desire out of his eyes, out of his voice. Pretending to look her over dispassionately, he said, "Do you have a slip on?"

She nodded, staring at him apprehensively.

He swallowed hard and forced himself to go on. "Half or full?"

"Half."

"Okay." He gestured toward her. "Drop your skirt."

Panic flared in her chest again. "No!"

He managed to keep his eyes hard and cold, but it was a major effort. "Either we do it this way, or I'll have to do it the old-fashioned way."

Instinctively she crossed her arms at her chest. "No. I'm not stripping in front of you."

His square jaw hardened. "Drop your skirt, or I'll have to come and take it off you."

She swallowed. Something in his voice sounded very sincere. She believed him. He would do what it took. She was going to have to compromise. After all, he seemed to be co-operating with her desperate effort to keep him from touching her. She supposed she would have to go halfway.

Avoiding his eyes, she unzipped her skirt and let it fall with a rustle to the ground. Her half-slip was peach colored and silky and it clung to her legs, but that was better than nothing at all. She stared at the far wall, not wanting to look into his face at the moment, and waited to see if he was satisfied yet.

"Okay. Lift your arms again and turn," he said, hoping she didn't notice the slightly hoarse quality that had crept into his voice.

Closing her eyes, she did as he asked, turning slowly, holding her breath.

This was bad police work and he knew it. Maybe it was the weather. Or maybe it was the way the two of them were forced to share this isolated piece of time and space with each other. Or maybe it was how long it had been since he'd felt a woman's touch, a woman's embrace. Or maybe it was just her. He didn't know, and right now, he didn't much care. He only knew he wanted her with an agonizing urgency that was tearing his body apart, and he had to resist it.

He couldn't do the body search, not now, not after what he'd felt just looking at her. And he knew he was taking a risk. What if she had a weapon hidden somewhere private? He looked at her hard, looked everywhere experience told him might be a hiding place, and tried to breathe evenly. He saw no sign of anything. Of course, she was such a pro, she could easily fool him. A groan tore his throat, though he wouldn't let it out. This was crazy. She could have all sorts of weapons hidden.

Hell, if she did, she did. And maybe she would kill him during the night, when his guard was down. Right now he knew he was going to have to risk it. Because he didn't dare touch her. Couldn't do it.

Still, there was one more thing. Once again he'd avoided something he should have done from the first. Glancing down at the information he had on her, he realized he'd been avoiding it for a very good reason. But he was at least going to have to let her know.

"Okay," he said crisply. "I don't see any evidence of weapons. So I'm going to trust you."

She beamed at him, grateful and triumphant, all in one. "Oh, thanks," she said sincerely, her pretty smile like the sun breaking through on a cloudy day. "I won't let you down."

The smile blew him away. It was the first time he'd had the brunt of its full force, and he had to turn from her, avoid looking into that smile the way one had to avoid looking into the sun. It was too bright, too embracing. He forced a frown to fight the effects.

"But while you're at it," he said gruffly. "Out of your...uh...clothes, I mean." God, if he didn't watch out, he'd be blushing next. "There's something else we could take care of."

She froze, staring at him. "What's that?"

He cleared his throat and shuffled papers. "Billie Joe Calloway has . . . well, she's got this identifying characteristic."

"Oh?" She waited for a moment, but it didn't seem he wanted to go on. "What is that?"

He shuffled papers again and she felt a spark of hope. What was wrong? Why didn't he want to tell her? Was it something that was going to easily prove that she wasn't the woman he was looking for? He just didn't want to be proved wrong, did he?

She gazed at him, almost eager. "What is this identifying characteristic?" Her eyes were shining now. "Quick, I can prove to you I don't have it. Then you'll know, and I can go free." It was all so simple. Why hadn't he brought this up before? She could think of a few bad names she would like to call him. But if this thing worked, all would be forgiven. As long as she was free to walk whenever she pleased, she didn't care how she got there.

He looked up and met her gaze, looking reluctant. "You really want to know?"

Did she want to know? She almost laughed aloud. "Oh, come on, Mr. Tough Guy. Tell me!"

His eyes narrowed but he held her gaze. "It seems Miss Calloway has a small, but rather fancy tattoo of a heart . . . on . . ." He took a deep breath. "On the left cheek of her derriere."

Cami paled. All laughter fled. All hope began to drain away. "You made that up," she said evenly, glaring at him.

He shook his head. "No, I didn't. It's true."

She stared a moment longer, then made a sound of exasperation. "Yes, you did. A tattoo on her . . . do you expect me to believe that for one minute?"

He ran his tongue quickly over his bottom lip to wet it, and looked at her again. "I don't care if you believe it."

"Oh, right." She tossed her hair. "And I suppose you expect me to reveal my . . . my . . ." She reddened despite herself. "Just so you can laugh at me."

He groaned, but it was inside. She couldn't hear it. He couldn't let her know the truth. If she got even a hint of how much power she had over him, he was a goner. She would run rings around him. He couldn't let that happen. "Believe me," he said softly, "I wouldn't laugh."

She folded her arms across her chest and looked at him defiantly. "Well, I'm not going to do it."

He felt a sense of relief. "I didn't think you would."

"Meaning . . . ?"

"Meaning, what percentage is there for you in doing it? If you show me blank skin, you prove your point. But since you won't show me . . ."

She clenched her hands into fists. "Oh!"

"Since you won't show me, I have to assume it is because you're afraid of incriminating yourself."

"Not at all." She stuck her chin out. "You see, it's like this. I'm not Billie Joe, and I could prove it to you by . . . by showing you. But what good would it do? I'd still be stuck here in the snow with you for the night. Wouldn't I?"

He nodded slowly. "But I wouldn't have to lock you up," he reminded her.

She hesitated. "You're not really going to do that," she said softly, her eyes luminous in the shadows of the corner where she stood.

"Of course I'm going to do it."

Didn't she understand the seriousness of all this? It was really her air of innocence more than anything else that made him think it might be possible she wasn't the woman in the warrant. Billie Joe had to be a hardened customer, and this young woman before him was anything but. Or so she seemed. Billie Joe might also be an expert at fooling people. He'd never met a woman that good at it, but that didn't mean she couldn't exist.

"So all you have to do is show me," he said softly, slowly, and then he watched her eyes.

She was tempted. She should do it. What the heck? This was the nineties, after all. No one was supposed to be hung up on those old body taboos anymore.

Yeah, nobody but her. She pictured the scene. She would pull down her slip and her underpants on that side. He would have to come closer, just to be sure. He might even reach out to push away some fabric. He might have to touch her, run his hand...

She shuddered, feeling suddenly itchy all over. She couldn't do it. There was no way. She shook her head, glancing into his eyes, then looking away. "No," she said. "I...I can't."

A feeling swept through him and he wasn't sure what it meant. It wasn't relief. How could it be? But it wasn't triumph, either. As far as he was concerned, this proved it. If she wouldn't show him what could clear her, she was obviously guilty. So much for the innocent act.

And now that he'd cleared that up, the ambivalent feelings he'd had, the attraction, the enigma—that should all fade away. She wasn't so mysterious after all. Just another con artist.

"Okay," he said crisply. "You can get dressed. I'll trust you on the rest."

She sighed, relieved, and reached for her skirt.

He knew he should turn away and busy himself with something to take his mind off what she was doing, but for some reason he seemed to be rooted to the spot. He watched her as she slid the skirt up and fastened it at the waistband, and then he heard his voice saying something he had neither planned nor expected.

"Except for one thing."

She turned and stared at him, frozen. "What?" she asked in dread.

He felt like a sleepwalker. He hadn't meant to say it, he hadn't meant to do it, even though he knew it should be done. And now he was committed. "Your hair," he said softly.

"My hair?" Her hand went to shove it back, as though she might hide it somehow.

"Yes. Your hair." Stepping toward her, he reached out and took hold of a handful and drew her closer. "You can hide all sorts of things in a nest like this," he murmured as he began to explore it.

And at the same time, he was cursing himself. Sure, it was something that needed to be done. But he knew he wasn't doing it because he really suspected she was hiding contraband in her hair. He was doing it because he craved the feel of her, because his hands wanted to feel her skin and his head wanted to fill himself with her scent and his body wanted to take hers in the most basic, primitive way a man could take a woman. And for giving in to that temptation, he cursed himself, and at the same time he fought his own instinctive nature, fought the pleasure it gave him to touch her in even such a simple way, fought the thrill it gave him to think of holding her, and tried to tell himself enough was enough.

It had all happened so fast, she hadn't had time to object, or even to pull away. A sound, like rushing water, filled her head and her mind went blank. He was so close. The top of her head came to his chin, and she was staring at his chest, staring at the button at the collar of his shirt, feeling his strong hands make their way through her hair, pushing aside the full weight of it as his fingers seemed to touch her in a strange, new, caressing way. She couldn't breathe. She felt as though she didn't need to. She was suspended in some sort of warm mist, and all she could see was khaki, all she could sense was his strength, so close.

She wanted that strength, wanted to hold it. In some dim, primordial instinct, deep inside, she wanted to curl into it, join her female need with his male power, feel his warm protection, feel his arms close in and hold her. There was an urgency to this need, a sense of inevitability, a compulsion to press herself to him, that was stronger than anything she'd ever felt well up inside her this way. She lifted her face, trying to see into his eyes, reaching for something . . .

A quiver of panic slashed through her. No, she had to pull back out of this. She had to distract them both, get the mood turned around. How was she going to do that? She thought quickly, but all she could come up with was a feeble joke.

"I think I've seen orangutans doing this," she said shakily, trying to smile.

"What?" he said, and at the same time, his fingers deepened their pressure on her sensitive scalp.

"Nothing," she murmured, giving up. What was the use? She couldn't pretend.

He hadn't really heard her. He was walking in quicksand, and he knew it, but he couldn't seem to dig himself out. She wanted him to kiss her. He could see it in her eyes, in the softening of her mouth, in the way her body swayed toward his. All he had to do was let it happen. It shouldn't happen. It couldn't happen. But it felt so right. It would come so naturally. His hand tightened against her head. One kiss. What could it hurt? Just one . . . and he began to pull her face toward his.

But it never got there, and the kiss didn't happen. A sudden gust of icy wind filled the room as the door was flung open and a large, dark man in a sheepskin parka burst in. Rafe still held her, though his head rose and he frowned at the intruder. But Cami twisted away, feeling suddenly shocked, suddenly guilty, as though she'd just been awakened from an erotic dream.

"Damn it, Sam," Rafe said gruffly, flexing his empty hands, missing her already. "You don't always have to come busting in like a grizzly, do you?"

"Hey." The tall Native American grinned, slamming the door and stamping his feet to get warm again. "It's my way. What can I tell you?"

Rafe was feeling uncharacteristically annoyed with his deputy. He was usually glad to see him, but right now, he was feeling deprived of something he'd wanted very badly.

He knew Sam had probably saved him from a situation that could have deteriorated rapidly if it had continued. But he didn't care right now. He just felt cheated.

"I thought you Navaho were supposed to be a little more subtle," he grumbled, glancing at Cami and wondering what she was thinking.

"We Navaho are straight shooters, man. Not like you sneaky Apaches." His wide grin softened the words that were obviously part of a long-running gag between them. But his grin faded as he took a good look at Cami. "And what have we got here?" he asked softly, his dark eyes taking in her frazzled look.

Rafe hesitated. His first impulse was to tell Sam to get lost. He wanted to handle this situation on his own. But once he'd reconnected with his brain, he realized that was impossible.

"I was just completing a search before locking her up," he told him.

"Oh yeah?" Sam's face didn't change, but Rafe knew he was thinking what he'd seen when he'd walked in had looked like something very different.

"I found her up on the old forest road. Take a look at this." He shuffled through the papers on his desk and found the information on Billie Joe, handing it to his deputy. "She was driving a green Mustang and had no identification on her."

Sam scanned the paper, looked up at Cami and whistled low. "You mean we finally got a real live criminal up here and you didn't call me in on it?"

Cami shook her head to clear it. She was still in a daze from what had just happened with this Neanderthal sheriff a moment ago. Or just about happened, she reminded herself. She'd lost her mind for a moment, but she had it back now.

"Are you a sheriff, too?" she asked the newcomer quickly.

"Uh, not exactly." Sam glanced at Rafe and back to Cami. "Just a sheriff wanna-be at this point," he added. "This guy here's my boss."

"Oh." Her shoulders sagged. "I'm trying to get some-one to pay some attention and realize that I'm not this Bil-lie Joe Calloway person. Your boss..." She jerked a thumb in Rafe's direction. "He saw me once, jumped to conclu-sions, and here I am, arrested." She stepped closer to the big man. "Do I look like a wild woman to you?" she de-manded. "Do I look like someone who would shoot up bars and con people out of their money?"

"Uh...no." Sam glanced at his boss apologetically. "Actually, that's the last thing you look like."

"You see?" Whirling, she gazed at Rafe jubilantly. "Everyone else can see it. Why can't you?"

Rafe groaned, slumping in his chair. "Sam, why are you here?" he asked with some annoyance.

The large man plunked himself down on the corner of the desk. "To tell you the truth, I came by to check on you. I was over at Naimo's when the electricity blew. I've got my snowmobile, so I thought I'd drop by Sally's and just see how she was doing with this storm and all."

"Good excuse," Rafe murmured cynically.

Sam grinned. "I thought so. But, anyway, I saw you had a lantern on over here and I figured you were working late, and by the way, Sally says to tell you she's keeping things hot for you, just in case." He shook his head, his mouth twisted with disdain. "Now that is one foxy lady and how you can keep stringing her along like you do, I don't know. If she invited me over for...ahem...hot coffee, I'd be there with bells on before she hung up the phone. But you...you just smile and tell her maybe next time and she gets that sad look on her face and..."

"And you stop by and try to cheer her up," Rafe inter-jected, but his face was feeling hot and he didn't dare look at Cami.

"Well, sure. I'm a nice guy." But he shook his head. "Listen, Rafe, Sally's ready and able to soothe that troubled brow of yours. You can't spend your life living with the ghost of a relationship that—"

Rafe rose abruptly, turning and almost squaring off against the other man, his face hard and unfriendly. "You also talk too much for a Navaho," he said harshly.

But Sam didn't take offense. His broad face was as calm and pleasant as ever. "I know. Everyone says that. But we're all that way in the Too Tall Clan. Can't help it. We're just born that way. We like to talk."

"And that's why you can't get a nice Navaho girl to marry you," Rafe noted coolly, still frowning at him.

"Well, there's always Sally," Sam retorted. "That is, if she ever gets over this stupid crush she's got on you."

Rafe's expression couldn't hide his exasperation. "Go home, Sam. I can handle this."

Sam slid off the desk, but he didn't seem to be in any hurry to leave. His glance took in Cami again, and he seemed to like what he saw. A new idea flashed across his friendly face. "Say, boss, listen. If you want to go home and get some rest, I could take over. You've been on duty all day. It doesn't seem fair that—"

"Go home, Sam."

Sam saluted with a finger to his forehead. "You got it, boss. I'm outa here."

Cami watched in frustration as the big man sauntered toward the door, the sheriff following him and giving him last-minute instructions in a voice too low for her to hear. Someone, somewhere, was going to have to listen to the truth and believe it. Her last hope of the evening was walking out. She'd never felt so helpless before in her life.

And at the same time, her heart was beating faster. She was about to be alone with this man again, and suddenly her mind was full of what had happened just before Sam had arrived. Was it going to happen again? Of course not. She wasn't going to let it. So why was she feeling more excited than apprehensive about that very prospect?

"The human psyche is a strange and intricate thing," she murmured to herself. "And completely untrainable, it seems." She might as well have said the human heart, and she knew it, but she wasn't ready to face that quite yet.

Four

Rafe wasn't sure what made him take out the picture of Janie and look at it. Maybe it was the way Sam had brought her up. Maybe it was something about Cami that reminded him. In any case, he suddenly had a need to look at it, to take it out and hold it. He never did that unless he was sure he was going to be alone for a good long time. He'd let Cami have some privacy in the bathroom, knowing it was completely secure and that there wasn't anywhere she could run to in the snow, anyway. But he couldn't predict how long she would be in there. Still, he took a chance.

The picture itself was getting pretty ragged. He'd had it in a frame, but the glass had broken and he hadn't replaced it. Somehow it had felt better in his hands without the glass in the way, warmer, closer, more accessible. But he knew it wouldn't last like this. The edges were fraying, and cracks were developing. The picture might not hold up much longer.

Still, he was pretty sure that wouldn't matter. Her face was burned into his mind anyway. Always would be. The smile, the bright brown eyes, the funny quirk at the corner of her mouth—every detail was a part of him. Always would be.

It had been three years, and it could have been yesterday. The rage still burned as hot in his gut, and the love still haunted his heart. What had Sam said—the ghost of an old relationship? But it wasn't that way at all. Janie was still so alive in his soul. And that was the way he wanted it.

He didn't hear Cami come out of the bathroom, didn't notice she'd rejoined him as she came up behind him silently and gazed at the picture for a moment over his shoulder.

"Who is it?" she asked.

He turned it quickly and slipped it back into his briefcase, all in one smooth move that took half a second. "Nobody," he said shortly.

But she'd seen the woman's sunny smile, seen how gentle his hands were holding the aging picture, and she suddenly remembered what Sam had said about his past.

"Are you married?" she asked abruptly, although she thought she already knew the answer from what Sam had said about somebody named Sally having a crush on him.

"No," he told her, swiveling in his chair to look at her. "Are you?"

The question surprised her and she almost laughed. "We've already been through that. But you're trying to trick me, aren't you?" she said impudently. "You're the one with the rap sheet on the legend of Billie Joe. You tell me. Is the old girl married or not?"

His dark eyes followed her every move. "My information doesn't say anything about any current marriage. I thought maybe you could fill me in."

"Well, let's see." She sank into a chair across the desk from him. "If I really were Billie Joe, I'd say she was the sort of gal who didn't need any one man to make her happy." She frowned, thinking. "In fact, she probably doesn't trust men much. That's why she's out there on her own, shooting up the countryside and making her own way in the world."

His mouth twisted in derision. "You make her sound like Annie Oakley."

"Why not? Maybe someday they'll be writing ballads about good old Billie Joe."

He considered that for a moment. "So you see her as a romantic figure?" he asked, watching her eyes as though he were prepared to gauge her response.

Another trick question. If she really was the evil one, she would certainly think of herself as a mythic figure, wouldn't she? Ha. She wasn't going to fall for this.

"Real crime is never really romantic," she said. "It's only the fake stuff off in the distance that some people think looks exciting."

He nodded slowly, making a bridge with his fingers. "Do you think she did it for the fame?"

"Fame?" Cami looked startled. "I never heard of her before you brought her up."

He stared at her for a long moment, wishing he could believe her. A part of him did. But the cop in him couldn't let go of the other part—the part that said, again and again, that it just wasn't likely there were two blondes running around these New Mexico mountains in green Mustangs. And her lack of identification was very suspicious. People didn't drive the byways without their licenses in this day and age. The purse-falling-out-in-the-snow story was hard to swallow.

But what if it were all true? What would he do if he decided she was innocent? That this was a case of mistaken identity?

He would have to let her go. But where could she go in this storm, anyway? There was no point in going out on a limb. No, they would both have to wait for morning to sort this thing out.

"Well," he said, rising and picking up his ring of keys. "It's about time we got on with it."

Cami looked at him, biting her lip. She'd been nervous about how they would be with each other once Sam left, but she might as well have saved herself the effort. He'd acted as though the almost-kiss had never happened. His gaze was cool, his shoulders set for business. She couldn't detect a hint of interest in her as a woman—only the scrutiny of a suspicious policeman who was watching her for signs of guilt. This was getting really old. She frowned at him, about to tell him so, when he stunned her with his next words.

"Get into the cell," he said, looking down at her.

The shock that ran through her body was almost electric. Her mouth went dry and she had trouble getting out her protest. "You... you can't put me in a cell."

His dark gaze didn't waver. "I can. And I will."

Her chin rose and she glared her defiance at him, despite the way her heart was beating. "You're going to have to pick me up and carry me."

He shrugged and took a step toward her. "Okay."

Rising, she backed away quickly. "No, wait a minute," she cried.

One dark eyebrow rose. "You mean you're going to walk in under your own power?"

She blinked at him, thinking fast. "Can't we work something out here?" she asked, trying not to show how anxious she was feeling. "I've been a good arrestee, haven't I? I mean, I haven't really tried to make a serious break for it. What makes you think I would do something like that?"

"Experience," he said simply, taking another step toward her.

"Wait, wait!" She shivered, not ready to admit defeat just yet. "What if I promise?" she insisted, taking another step back.

He shook his head. "Believe me, we'll both feel much more secure with you locked in for the night."

Locked in for the night. The words chilled her blood. She turned to look at the stark, ugly cell and began to face exactly what that meant—the small, hard cot, the bars, the loneliness.

"You're not..." She was horrified as the prospect grew closer to reality. She turned and met his hard gaze with wide eyes of her own. "You're not going to lock me up in that cage and then go off and leave me, are you?"

Of course he was. Or at any rate, he should. A muscle twitched at his jawline. What did she think he was, a social worker? He was a cop, for God's sake. He'd arrested her on suspicion of being a person whose activities branded her as a menace to society. Didn't she get it? It was definitely time she faced reality and stopped trying to con him with this innocent act.

But for some reason, that wasn't what came out of his mouth when he finally replied. Instead, he heard himself saying gruffly, "I'm not leaving right away. I've got a couple hours of paperwork still to do."

Not good enough, she thought anxiously. That still left her behind bars. She couldn't let that happen. Stall. She had to stall.

Turning to face him, she set her hands on her hips and looked at him accusingly. "Are you trying to tell me it's just going to be you and me in here almost all night?"

He hesitated. That would teach him not to try to do good deeds. If he'd kept his mouth shut, he could be on his way to his own bed within the hour. Instead, he'd opted to stay here with her, and now she was making that seem ominous. She had a way of turning a phrase to put the strangest spin on it.

But basically she had the picture. "That's right," he said, his scowl challenging her to make something out of it.

She frowned at him. "But, I could..." She shrugged, thinking fast. "I could claim sexual harassment or something."

Silently he groaned. Here we go again. Shades of the big city, just as he'd suspected. "You could claim it," he said harshly. "But you'd be lying."

She sniffed. "Well, that remains to be seen."

"No, it doesn't." He had the hardest eyes she'd ever seen, and when he took another step toward her, her heart skipped a beat and she retreated again, unable to stifle a tiny gasp of alarm.

He could move more quickly than she could, and before she realized what was happening, he had her wrist in his grasp. "Are you telling me that besides being a burglar, a bunco artist, and a fugitive from justice, you're a liar?" he asked her coldly.

She tried to keep up a defiant front with sarcasm, but it came out wobbly. "Oh, no. Heaven forbid."

"Good. Then we understand each other," he said evenly as he led her toward the cell.

She wanted to shrink back, but she steeled herself and tried to breathe evenly, calmly. It was about time she settled down and stopped being silly. No matter how she felt about this, it was going to happen. If she wanted to fly off the handle and get hysterical, she would only succeed in embarrassing herself. It was time to put this all into proper perspective. When life handed you lemons, you tried to invent a new recipe for lemonade. Anything else was self-defeating.

"I can walk by myself," she told him, yanking her hand away from his. And she did, holding her head up high.

But entering the cell still spooked her, despite her best intentions. The air seemed colder, the floor harder. A sliver of panic slid down her spine and she turned quickly, stopping him before he closed her inside.

"Wait a minute," she said, feigning indignation. "This cell is gross."

He glanced around it and looked back at her, not fooled a bit. "It's clean."

She folded her arms and bit her lip. "How do you know? Did you clean it yourself?"

"No. But I supervised the people who did."

She looked around uneasily, wishing she could find something specific to complain about. "Gee, that's so reassuring."

He knew she was stalling, but for some reason he didn't really mind. He leaned against the bars and watched her from under lowered lids. "It's the nicest jail in this part of the state. Believe me."

She glanced at him and began to pace nervously. "Why should I?"

He almost smiled. "Because you don't have much of a choice, do you?"

She paced from one side of the limited space to the other, and it only took her three steps to do it. "It looks like a closet with bars on the door," she complained, throwing out her arms experimentally. She couldn't quite touch both sides at once, but the point was made.

"It's small," he conceded. "We don't get much call to use it." He watched her pace for a moment, then added, a touch of humor stirring in his voice, "We don't get too many criminals like you in town."

Whirling, she faced him. "I'll bet you don't." She saw the amusement in his eyes and found herself trying to maintain a balance between wanting to coax out a real smile and wanting to punch him in the nose.

"This is a game to you, isn't it?" she demanded. "You're having a ball watching me squirm."

He didn't answer, but the merriment sparkled a little more brightly.

Her chin rose, eyes narrowing accusingly. "I'll bet you haven't had this much excitement since . . . since . . ."

"Since Harry Moon dropped acid," he interjected helpfully, "and thought he was an eagle. We had to lock him in here to keep him from trying his wings off the roof of the Veterans' building." He looked thoughtful. "That was last July, if I remember right."

In a gesture of exasperation, she lifted her hands. "Gee, then I guess I really am the biggest criminal you've had in here for years, aren't I?"

He nodded, watching her. "You got it."

She turned and paced restlessly, and then faced him again. "What's next? Is the reporter from the local paper going to be in here to ask me how I got started on my road to a life of crime? Is the TV station going to interview people in the street as to my guilt or innocence? Are you going to take a poll as to whether I should get the death penalty?"

He shrugged, forcing back the smile that threatened once again to take over his habitually stern look. "Could be."

He was infuriating. "Well, hot diggity," she said, sarcasm dripping from her tongue. "I guess I'm a real celebrity at last."

"Could be." And finally he smiled.

It was a real smile. It reached his eyes. White teeth flashed against his dark skin, and a genuine warmth appeared and flooded her with something hot and sparkling. Stopping in her tracks, she stared at him, mouth slightly open.

As quickly as it had appeared, his smile evaporated and he turned abruptly, reaching for his keys, ready to lock her in.

She saw the move and caught her breath in her throat, all her bravado gone in an instant. "Don't lock the door. Please. I . . . I promise I won't try to get out. Honest. Just don't lock it."

He hesitated, struck by the sincere distress he read in her eyes. Not locking the cell defeated the whole purpose of using it, but he found himself drawing back and putting the keys into his pocket. "Okay," he said coolly. "Just as long as you behave yourself."

But he had to turn away so she wouldn't see the look in his eyes. He was just as reluctant to lock her in as she was to have him do it. Somehow the picture of her behind bars stuck in his craw. He'd never felt this way about an arrest he'd made before. Why now? Why her?

Turning his back on the cell, he tried to block it from his mind as he returned to his desk and pulled out papers to deal with. But the pages blurred in front of him. He couldn't concentrate. His mind was still back in that cell, and he didn't like it. Why couldn't he lock her up like he should? Why?

Maybe he was just getting soft in his old age. Maybe it was the territory. After all, he didn't make many arrests up here. Maybe he'd lost the knack, lost the anger.

Yeah, that was what he would like to believe. But he knew better. It was her. Something about her wouldn't leave him alone. Something about her was eating away at his rigid self-possession. He was caught up in a crazy and very inappropriate attraction to her, and he might as well face it. He was like a damn kid with a teenage crush.

But at the same time, why did memories of Janie keep floating into his mind? Ordinarily he was very careful not to think about her while he was on the job, or anytime he was with other people. He saved her for the quiet hours, the moments just before he fell asleep, the early mornings when he went out and saw the dew on the flowers, or watched the first snowfall send its crystal magic across the yard. That was when he let her image fill his mind. That was when she felt close, almost alive again. Sometimes it brought a lump to his throat to have her that near. And sometimes it filled him with happiness. He was never sure beforehand which it would be. She had a life of her own in his heart. She was still just as unpredictable as ever.

The front door banged open again. Sam was back, carrying a cardboard box and fighting back the snow. "Chow's on," he called, striding straight toward the cell where Cami sat forlornly on her skinny cot. "Hope you're hungry."

"What?" She stood, astounded. "You brought me food?"

"Sure did." The tall Navaho noted with surprise that the cell was unlocked. Glancing at Rafe before he looked at Cami again, he widened his eyes in reaction but had the good sense not to comment. Walking on in, he set the box down on the chair. "Mrs. Cummins, the lady next door, she cooks for our...prisoners." Suddenly he looked uncomfortable with the concept as well. "Rafe told me to stop by and get you something to eat. So here it is."

"Oh!" It was like a miracle. There was nothing like food to revive spirits, and she felt a wave of relief, drinking in the scent of it as though the smell alone would nourish her. "Fried chicken and mashed potatoes and gravy and succotash. And..." She pulled out a thermos and unscrewed the lid. "Tea!" She stood staring at it, hardly hearing Sam as he went on.

"Yeah, usually we just give the prisoners coffee, but Rafe said you needed tea, so I—"

"Thanks, Sam," Rafe interrupted, herding his deputy toward the door. "Go on home and get some rest. I can handle things from here on out."

"Okay," the big man agreed cheerfully. "Hey, Billie Joe," he called back just before opening the door out into the storm. "Hope you can prove your innocence tomorrow. Good luck."

She smiled, waving. "Thanks, Sam. I appreciate the vote of confidence. But the name is Cami."

Her smile faded as the door closed behind the Navaho and Rafe turned back into the room. Avoiding his gaze, she sat down on the cot and began setting up her chair as a table, arranging the food. She really wasn't very hungry, but it smelled so good, and the tea was a lifesaver. A real lifesaver. And it also confused her.

She'd mentioned tea in one of her petulant rantings, and he'd remembered. He'd told Sam to make sure she got what she wanted. As she sat back and sipped from the thermos top, her cheeks felt hot and she knew, though the tea was warm, it wasn't from that.

Rafe Lonewolf, that mean, horrible Neanderthal sheriff who'd treated her so rudely—that very same man had made a thoughtful gesture that touched her. He'd noticed what she wanted and acted upon it. How many men ever did that?

Not many. Leaning back, she listened to the wind howling around the building and thought it over. Finally she risked looking up to see what he was doing. Sitting at his desk again, he seemed to be going over some sort of ledger.

"Would you like some of this food?" she asked him. "There's plenty. And I'm not really very hungry."

"No, thanks," he said shortly, not looking up. "I ate earlier."

She gnawed on a chicken wing and took a few bites of the mashed potatoes, not because she really wanted the food, but more because she hated to think of all that work gone to waste for Mrs. Cummins. The food was warm and very tasty. She packed everything back in the box, except for the thermos of tea. That she kept with her.

"Well, what do we do now?" she asked him once she was finished organizing things.

He did glance at her, but only for a moment. "You do whatever you want. I've got some reports to fill out."

She sighed, watching his hand move with the pen across the paper. "Reports? I thought there wasn't any crime in this town."

He glanced her way again. "That's what I'm reporting," he said, and she could have sworn he almost smiled again.

"Hey, I just thought of something," she said in a blatant attempt to keep his attention. "You're sitting here without any phone service. You're supposed to be the local law enforcement. How can anybody call you if something goes wrong somewhere?''

"They'd just send somebody over. Half the people in this area don't have phones anyway. It doesn't make that much of a difference.''

The concept of a world without telephones boggled her city-bred mind. She thought of her fax machine, her modem, her cellular phone and every other toy of the communications industry that she'd embraced in recent years and shook her head. "You're kidding.''

"No. People existed for centuries without phones, you know. It can be done.''

"I can't even imagine it.''

He turned in his chair and dropped his pen. She felt a glow of accomplishment as he went on.

"A hundred years ago, when this building was built, nobody out here had phones. But everyone had a horse, and could ride quickly to the next farm to report an accident or a crime. Things got taken care of.''

"Did you grow up here?'' she asked, leaning forward.

"No.'' He shook his head. "I grew up in Phoenix and Albuquerque and L.A. I've only lived out here in the sticks for the last three years.''

"What made you move all the way out here?'' She was really interested this time, not just playing at forming a friendship. She knew it was incongruous, asking questions and chatting, as though they weren't the mortal enemies they'd seemed like all night, fighting over whether or not she was a very bad person. It was surreal, but besides being a way to pass the time, she had to admit—she was interested.

He hesitated for a few seconds, as though he thought it strange to talk like this, too. But then he seemed to accept it, for he answered slowly and didn't brush her off. "I got tired of things in the city. The intensity. The ugliness. I wanted to come out to someplace fresh and clean, where people still believe in each other."

"The idyllic, pastoral life." She smiled, surprised at this side of him. "Did you find it? Or is that dream a hoax, like we city people always tell ourselves it is?"

"I like it here," he said, by way of an answer. "It's a good life."

She shook her head slowly, thinking of his answer earlier when she'd asked what he did for fun. "I would go nuts," she admitted. "I don't think I could take it."

His mouth twisted. "Yeah, you're probably right," he responded. "Not much scope for your sort of life-style out here."

She knew right away he was talking about Billie Joe, not about Cami Bishop, and she resented it. Just when she thought they were finally making a breakthrough, he had to go and dredge up that again.

"I don't know how I'm going to get this through to you," she said with fire in her gaze, "since you just refuse to listen, but I am not this crazed *bandido* woman running around the countryside shooting the place up like you think I am. I'm a very conventional woman. I want the same things every other conventional woman wants."

He leaned way back in his chair and his grin was slow and knowing. "Oh, now you're going to tell me you're hankering after a white picket fence and a baby carriage. Is that right?"

"You got it. That's exactly what I want." She shrugged. "It looks like that's not what I'm going to get," she added softly, then turned and said more loudly, "but it's what I've always wanted. Just in the city. Not out in the boonies."

"Give it a few years," he murmured, his eyes glazing in a way that let her know his attention was drifting back and away from her. "You might change your mind."

She watched him for a moment, watched memories flicker behind his eyes. "What made you change your mind?" she asked him at last. She'd noticed a slight limp earlier when he walked. "Were you wounded?"

He looked up as though he were startled to find her still there. Then the wall came down behind his eyes, his features froze in the emotionless mask she already knew so well, and he turned away.

"I've got to get these reports finished," he said gruffly, picking up the pen.

In a sudden flash of inspiration, she realized his reaction had something to do with the picture she'd found him staring at, but she knew better than to ask any questions about it. Instead, she sat in silence and watched him work while she sipped her tea.

In a grotesque way, she was almost content, for the moment. At least she was inside, out of the storm. In the morning she would be able to prove her innocence and be on her way to the baby shower. In the meantime, this wasn't really such a bad place to spend some time. It was certainly better than her car would have been, stranded at the side of the road.

She shivered, thinking about it. It really had been crazy to take off into the mountains like she had. Just that afternoon, she'd been having a nice lunch in a Santa Fe restaurant with Jules and Dr. Juan, two of the botanists who sometimes supplied humorous articles to her journal. Living in the high desert as they did, they were more interested in cacti and succulents than in ferns, but she loved their sense of humor and used their pieces for a change of pace now and then. They'd been horrified to hear of her plan to head north to Denver.

"There's a storm forecast," Jules had said. "Better stay with us tonight."

Storm, shlorm. She was a California girl. What did she know about storms? Tell her an earthquake was rumbling and she knew to prop herself up in a doorway and stay away from glass. But a snowstorm? Surely she would be able to drive on through. After all, what was the modern highway system good for if not for that?

"If you must go," Dr. Juan had told her, "maybe you can beat it. I hear it's not really going to get nasty until midnight or so. Now I know a little shortcut that will take you through the mountains, but it cuts about an hour off your travel time if you do it right."

Obviously she hadn't done it right. Anxious to get to Sara's a few days before the shower so they could have a good long talk before the others arrived, she'd pressed on. And ended up arrested.

It was funny, really. She never would have dreamed this could happen. It wasn't as though crazy things didn't happen to her all the time—they very definitely did. But they were usually little things, like losing her way and ending up having tea with a parish priest or finding a lost dog and dating its owner. Nothing as big or dangerous as this had ever happened to her before. There had been moments, a little earlier, when she'd actually begun to be afraid she might end up in a real jail somewhere, paying for Billie Joe's crimes with her own skin. But that wasn't going to happen. She was pretty sure things would be cleared up first thing the next day. And staying here really wasn't all that horrible— as long as she was released in the morning.

"Would you like any of this tea before I close the thermos back up?" she asked him.

He glanced at her. "No thanks," he said.

She twisted the cup onto the thermos and set it aside. "That was very nice of you," she said, feeling suddenly shy. "To have Sam get me the tea, I mean."

"It had nothing to do with nice," he said, turning and looking at her. "That's the way we treat prisoners here in New Mexico. We take good care of them."

"Anything they want, huh?"

"Not exactly." He stood, putting away files. "But we like to keep our perps happy."

A joke. He was making a joke. But she still had a problem with being called a perpetrator.

"Yeah, I'll just bet you do. And don't think we crims don't appreciate it," she said airily. "After all, we crims have to depend on the kindness of strangers an awful lot."

He turned around completely, staring at her. "Crims?" he repeated, his mouth twisting derisively as he said the word. "What the hell's a 'crim'?"

Ha. She had him there. "Short for criminal, of course," she told him pertly. "I can make up ridiculous nicknames, too."

He was going to laugh. There—she saw the evidence. But he stifled it and turned away, and she sighed. There was a sensual attraction between the two of them that couldn't be denied, but it seemed he was going to pretend it didn't exist. And maybe that was for the best. Maybe...

She leaned back against the pillow, watching him and wondering why she was feeling so peaceful, so serene. It had something to do with him, she realized suddenly. There was something in his strength, his hard reliability, that made her feel safe. She liked his hands, the way he held a pen, the way his head tilted toward the light of the lantern. Crazy, but in a strange way, she felt protected here.

As her eyes drifted shut, she still watched him, and in the soft space between wakefulness and sleep, she dreamed he held her in his arms.

Five

—————

Rafe's back was stiff from sitting in one position for so long, but he didn't want to move. From where he sat, he had the perfect view of his prisoner as she slept. He could watch the way her golden hair fell in waves against the pillow, the way the lantern light played along the creases of her silk blouse, showing just the curve of her breast, the long, slim line of her neck. He'd pulled the scrawny blanket over her after she'd fallen asleep and wished it were something full and fluffy.

Protective feelings—yes, he'd been having those. But he could handle things. He wasn't going to let it get out of hand. He knew better. He'd been there.

Been there—done that.

Janie's face swam into his mind again. She'd had a smile like a kid hiding a puppy in her jacket—half shy, half mischievous, and all warmth and fun. He remembered the day she'd been assigned to be his partner. He'd groaned when he saw her. She'd looked too short, too slight, too young. But it hadn't taken long for her to show him where her talents lay. She was tough and she could bluff street kids with the best of them. But what she was really good at was calming women in hysterics and men on the verge of mayhem. A word from Janie, a touch of her hand, and people quieted. Some folks had a special talent for making animals trust them. With Janie, it was people.

And she'd done the same with him, he realized with a rueful grin. She'd calmed him in no time, and pretty soon, she'd done more than that. He'd loved her like he'd never dreamed he could love another human being. She was everything to him—the first woman he'd ever been close to, if you didn't count his mother.

She'd wanted to get married. He'd held off, wary. Marriage was a big commitment. She'd talked about babies. And he'd been even more leery. There was too much ugliness in the world for him to be sanguine about bringing kids into it. What if their kids had turned out like these gang kids he had to deal with every day?

"That won't happen," she'd assured him solemnly. "We'll raise our kids with love and discipline and values. We won't let the street take them. We'll fight."

She was a fighter, all right. But in the end, she lost the only battle that really counted. And she'd left him all alone.

He'd been alone a lot in his life, so he should have been used to it. His mother had died when he was fifteen, and his father had taken off soon after, leaving him with his aunt. A college librarian, she'd worked all day and left him pretty much to his own devices, but she'd also brought home books, and that had opened a new world for him, filled his nights with adventures and concepts that had been so interesting to him, he hadn't hung out with the street kids, hadn't gotten into much trouble. That came later, in college, but it didn't last long. The party scene was boring to him. Books had always been better. He'd had few close friends, few girl friends, until Janie.

She'd changed his life. She'd taught him how to laugh, how to love, how to enjoy a sunset. He still had all that. She'd given it to him like a gift, and he would never give it up, because giving it up would mean giving away a piece of Janie.

There was a crackle, and suddenly the lights were on again. A glance at the clock told him it was almost three in the morning. He was tired, but wired at the same time. Something was flowing through his veins like adrenaline, and he couldn't relax. And he couldn't stop staring at the blonde in the cell.

She wasn't Billie Joe Calloway, was she? He couldn't be sure until he had the confirmation from a positive source, but he was getting pretty sure. And once he'd admitted that to himself, he had to wonder how he'd ever thought she was. After all these years as a cop, his instincts should have told him the truth. Why had he let himself be fooled for so long?

He almost felt it had to be something psychosomatic. Maybe he'd been out here in the sticks too long, so far away from real crime he hardly knew what it looked like anymore. Or maybe . . . maybe he was just lonely, and one look at her gorgeous face . . .

Okay, so she was attractive. She had a pretty enough face, and a body that sent his pulse pounding. But that was all your basic physical reaction. What counted was in the head. The body was just a primitive animal, when you came right down to it. See a nicely grilled steak and the saliva started forming. See a beautiful woman and the appropriate body parts went into readiness mode. So what? It didn't mean a thing.

Except that he'd been alone a long, long time, he reminded himself.

"And you're going to stay that way," he told himself aloud. "So watch it."

Easier said than done. No matter what he told himself, he knew he was going to stay right where he was, watching her. And that was asking for it.

Cami stirred and put her arm up over her eyes. Something was bothering her, something. . . .

She opened her eyes and stared at the room, shocked. For just a moment, she thought she must be dreaming. But then she remembered. No, this was no dream. This was quite definitely a nightmare. She was in jail. Jail! Impossible, but true.

A sound drew her attention and she found the sheriff standing over her cot, her thermos in his hands.

"Hi," he said, looking down at her. He'd seen her stir and had told himself to get out of the cell, on the double. But he hadn't listened. He wasn't going to listen. He was going to walk the tightrope, and he knew it.

"The lights are on," she noted, blinking up at him.

He nodded. "They came on about fifteen minutes ago. I was just putting away the food in the little refrigerator." That was his excuse for coming into the cell. The real reason, of course, was to be closer to her, to hear her breathing, as well as see the steady rise and fall of her chest.

To torture himself. That was about it. Good Lord, he was a fool. But he couldn't seem to stop being one.

"Okay." She struggled into a sitting position and pushed her hair back away from her face. Though the lights were on in the rest of the room, her corner cell was dark, almost as dark as it had been when the lantern was all the light they had. He stood over her silently, his face hidden by shadows, and she felt a tiny shiver steal down her spine.

But it wasn't fear she felt. No, not for a moment. Frowning slightly, trying to analyze the sensation, she realized what it was. Anticipation. That was it. And with the realization, a soothing warmth filled her, and she could sense herself relax.

He could sense it, too, and he knew he was playing with fire, just by staying so close to her. He hadn't meant to wake her, hadn't meant to let this attraction take hold like this. But it had. He was here, and it was as though he were being pulled in by a whirling vortex. He had to look at her, draw her in, every aspect of her. If he could just pull himself away...

But how was he going to do that when she looked so damn adorable, sitting there, her eyes sleepy, her hair tousled about her head, her blouse twisted so that her breasts were emphasized by the tight fabric—full, round, lovely breasts that he ached to touch?

Just a few more seconds, he told himself. Then he would go.

"You ought to go back to sleep," he told her softly. "It's only a little after three."

Still groggy, she nodded. She laid her head back down on the pillow, looking up at him with narrowed eyes, trying to make out his features in the gloom. "You haven't slept at all," she said drowsily.

He shrugged, and she shook her head. "What are you, some kind of vampire?" she asked, then felt a smile tugging at the corners of her mouth. A vampire—that would fit right in with the nightmare theory, wouldn't it? "Do you haunt the night and avoid all contact with the sun?"

"You're half-asleep," he told her, and then, to her surprise, he leaned down and adjusted her covers, the back of his hand brushing the bare skin of her arm.

She snuggled against the pillow but didn't take her eyes off him. Despite the power being back on, there was an eerie, dreamlike quality to the light, and as he bent over her, she felt the beating of her heart speed.

"You're tucking me in," she murmured, her eyes drifting shut. "You know how to make a prisoner feel right at home, don't you?"

He didn't answer, but he didn't leave, either. Suddenly she sensed that he was closer, and she opened her eyes to see why.

He was touching her hair, lacing his fingers through it and staring at the way its golden sheen caught the light. She lay very still, hardly breathing, and when he looked into her eyes, he saw that they were wide and observant. He paused, wondering what she was thinking. But he didn't take his hand away.

"What do you do to make your hair frizz up like that?" he asked her, a trace of a smile in his dark eyes.

"I'm sorry you don't like it," she said breathlessly, reaching up with her hand to cover his. "It's natural."

His hand turned, the fingers curling around hers, and he felt the jolt that went through him as he sensed how warm she was. But he made sure his eyes didn't show what he was feeling. And his words were casual, bantering, belying the way his pulse was beginning to race. "Natural. Right," he said sardonically. "And so's that golden color you've made it."

She stared up at him, her eyes filled with mysterious mists. She might be half-asleep, but she was very much aware of where this was going. Aware, and accepting. He could see it in her face. "I'm blond. Is there a law against being a blonde in this town?"

He hesitated, knowing he should leave, telling himself so inside. But he couldn't go. Not yet. Instead, he sank to sit on the cot beside her, drawn by a force too strong to resist. "Could be. I haven't checked the code lately."

"Better check it," she murmured, turning her face into the cup of his hand and closing her eyes. "Because if there is, I'm going to have to plead guilty."

His hand caressed her cheek. He felt dizzy. There was a roaring in his ears. She was soft and sweet to touch, and he knew she would be even sweeter to kiss. Sweet—but with a kick that promised to send him over the edge. "Don't worry,'' he told her, his breath coming more quickly. ''I'll get you out on a plea bargain.''

''You will?'' Her lips parted and her chin rose toward him. ''How can I ever thank you?'' she whispered, her eyes half-open, her body in a stretch she hadn't planned, wouldn't admit to, but one that was meant to convey a very specific message.

His hands tightened on her and he drew her to him as he bent to meet her. She was sweet, just as he'd known she would be, but sweet like brandy, like fine cognac, with a deep, wild taste that made him more thirsty even as he drank in all he could get of her. He'd meant to be gentle, but by the time their lips touched, his head had given up on logic, on plans. Feeling was what took over, desire, need, urgency. She melted in his arms like wax, taking him in, curling around him. He pulled her closer, harder, his mouth moving on hers, exploring, demanding, searching for something he couldn't name.

She gasped, surprised, shocked, even. She'd wanted him to kiss her. She'd realized she was attracted to him before she'd fallen asleep. She hadn't thought much of it. She was often attracted superficially. It was when you got to know most men that they turned up a day late and a dollar short. Over the past few years, she'd become used to enjoying the feeling of attraction without acting on it. Acting on it always led to disappointment. It was more fun just to live the dream.

But this—this was different. This was like jumping in a lake and discovering it harbored hot springs, like turning on the shower and finding yourself standing under a gusher of champagne. She'd never been kissed like this before, never been left breathless, heart pounding, head swimming. Far from disappointing, this was downright scary. It took over her head, jump-started her heart and filled her with a fire that threatened to run wild. Nothing had ever sent her reeling like this. But she didn't want it to stop.

Reaching up, she wrapped her arms around him, pulling him even closer, marveling at how natural it felt to need him this way.

You barely know this man, her mind was trying to telegraph through the sensual fog she was swimming in. *He thinks you're a criminal. He hasn't really been very nice.*

Go away, her heart responded. *Go away and let me live.*

"What?" Rafe thought she'd said something. He pulled his head back and looked down at her, only half-sane at the moment, but still aware enough to be careful. "What did you say?"

"Nothing," she murmured, touching his cheek with her hand. "I . . . nothing."

He looked down at her, stunned, like a man finally coming up for air. She was so beautiful with her golden hair spread out around her, a shimmering cloud of curls that framed her face. Her lips looked swollen from their kisses, her eyes were drowsy with desire. Her blouse had come open and one breast was exposed, its nipple dark and tight beneath the transparent lace of her bra. Something twisted inside him, twisted and contracted. He wanted her like he'd never wanted a woman before, the need like a force of nature within him, something he would have a hard time denying, like standing against a hurricane wind or braving a river during spring thaw.

But as he looked down at her, he saw what she was, and more important, who she wasn't. Her blond hair was so different from Janie's short, dark tresses. Her body was full and soft, where Janie had been slim and hard. As he looked, his hands stopped caressing and balled into fists, and he drew back, away from her, surprised.

He'd always told himself there would never be another woman like Janie. And yet here he was, responding to Cami this way. He hated to admit it, but Cami was special. She wasn't Janie, but she was special. Still, he had to resist the way he was feeling.

Swearing under his breath, he jackknifed away from her and turned, striding from the cell. She half rose, staring after him, confused. "What is it?" she asked him. "Did I...?"

"You didn't do anything," he said, turning back abruptly and wincing as he looked at her. He turned away again, quickly. If he looked too long, he wasn't sure he could stay away. "It's not you. It's me."

It was him all right. She hadn't done anything. But what he'd done was unprofessional at best, and possibly even criminal. He should never have touched her. He should never have let his thoughts translate into actions.

He risked a glance to see how she was taking his retreat. She was sitting very still, her eyes very wide. Groaning, he turned away again and cursed the impulse that had sent him up on the old forest road that evening. If only he'd gone to see Sally instead.

"Can I get out of my cell?" she asked suddenly.

He turned again, frowning fiercely. "Why do you want to do that?"

No longer waiting for permission, she rose, padding on stocking feet. "I need my jacket. It's a little cold in here."

He looked at her sharply, wondering if that was a shot at him, but her eyes were guileless. He picked up the little linen jacket to the suit, ready to hand it to her as she exited the cell and came walking toward him.

"I...I'm sorry about what happened in there," he began awkwardly. "It was very unethical of me. It shouldn't have happened."

She gazed into his face. "Why?" she asked, not ready to give him the easy way out. "Why not?"

He stared at her, not sure if she didn't get it, or was just being argumentative. "Because you're my prisoner, of course. I had no right to touch you."

"Ah." Head to the side, she gave him a wise look. "Well then, I guess you've got a decision to make. If I'm just boring old Cami Bishop, you can kiss me with impunity." She raised one eyebrow. "But if I'm really that exciting outlaw Billie Joe Calloway, kissing me might be grounds for getting you suspended. Is that about it?"

He stared at her for a moment, and then a lopsided grin began to appear. "You're certainly crafty enough to be an outlaw," he said softly, shaking his head. "You've got it all figured out."

She just smiled.

He sobered. "But you're only half-right," he said. "Even if you are the demure Miss Bishop, innocent and pure as the driven snow, I had no right to bother you like that. And I'm sorry."

She made a face. "I'm not sorry," she told him, her gaze calm and steady as it met his. "I liked it."

He swallowed, looking away. "Then you're not going to bring me up on sexual harassment charges after all?" he said.

She stared, frowning. "Is that what you're worried about?" But no. She could see it in his eyes. That wasn't what was bothering him at all. It was something else, and she had a feeling she knew what that might be.

It was a shame, because he was... She glanced at him again as she turned so that he could help her into her jacket. He was gorgeous. Why hadn't she noticed from the first? Probably because she'd been too busy being a smart aleck, and then being enraged. It wasn't that he was handsome, exactly. But he was clean and rough and strong, with a profile that could do a nickel proud. There was something about him that was incredibly compelling. In just a few hours, she would be cleared, and she would be on her way. And she would never see him again. That seemed a shame. But if he didn't feel the same way, there was no point to pursuing it.

Shrugging into her jacket, she felt something in the pocket. Reaching in, she came up with a crumpled envelope. The invitation.

"Look!" she cried, waving the piece of paper in front of his face and laughing with sudden joy. "Here's the invitation to Sara's baby shower. Look at the name and address on the envelope. Cami Bishop. You see?"

He gave it a glance and nodded. "So that's where you got the name," he noted cynically.

She gasped and sputtered and wanted to grab him by the collar and shake him into acknowledging the truth. But he was hardly listening. Instead, he was mulling over the fact that evidence was piling up, one bit after another. What if she really wasn't Billie Joe Calloway? What then?

Hell, who was he trying to kid? He knew she wasn't a fugitive. He'd known it for a long time now. But he'd gone this far, he really couldn't back down until he had definitive evidence to prove her innocent. And in the meantime, they had the better part of the night to kill. He had a restless feeling that he knew wasn't going to give him any peace. He was feeling claustrophobic, penned in, restricted—as though he were the one who was the prisoner. There had to be a better way. Glancing up at the window, he had an idea.

"You want to go outside and see the new snowfall?"

"In the storm?" But even as she said the words, she realized the wind was no longer lashing out at the building.

"Storm's over," he told her, gesturing for her to look at the window. Then he turned her way again, something eager lighting his eyes. "Want to go out and take a look?"

She smiled at him, relieved. Maybe they were going to weather this situation after all. "Can you trust me?" she taunted him playfully. "If I'm really the rootin', tootin' shootin' gal you think I am, won't I make a run for it?"

He gave her another of those grins she was beginning to get addicted to. "I'll risk it."

She smiled, more to herself than to him. "Okay. If you've got a warm coat I can borrow."

He had more than that. It took another half hour to get ready to go out, but once in the open air, she was happy to be encased in a down jacket, fur-lined boots a few sizes too big, gloves, a scarf, and a warm wool hat that she pulled down over her ears. She felt like a walking mummy, and it made her laugh to take giant steps in the new snow with those outsize boots, but she was warm. And once she'd acclimatized and begun to look around her, she was also enchanted.

New snow. The trees were shining icicles, planted in powdered sugar fields. Snowflakes caught the moonlight like diamonds, sparkling everywhere. The air was cold and fresh and delicious to breathe. The snow reflected the light of the moon, making everything so bright it was almost like daylight. At first, she hardly dared to move, but once she got going, every step she took made a deep, clean imprint in the snow. Laughing with delight, she ran, then fell clumsily and laughed some more.

He pulled her up. "Come on. This way."

They slogged their way through the snow. She got tired before he did and he made her walk in his footprints to save energy. They passed a little house and she realized they were out in the world while others were sleeping. Somehow that seemed so darn intimate she turned to him, wanting to kiss him or hold him close. But with all the clothing between them, she knew that wouldn't work, and she started to laugh again, struck by the wonderful silliness of it all.

He had no idea what she was laughing about, but he grinned at her and took hold of her hand. "Come on. There's a great hill up around the bend."

The hill was a long, sweeping span of perfect snow, lined with evergreens whose branches were creaking under the heavy white load each carried. With the carpet of snow below, the inky sky above, and the stars all sparkling in the moonlight, it looked like a fairyland. She held her breath, hardly believing anything could be so beautiful.

She laughed out loud, and he turned to her, surprised, and then basking in her warmth. "What's so funny?"

"I was just thinking about little kids in snowsuits. You know, all bundled up so that their arms stick straight out. Wouldn't they have fun here, sliding in the snow? Can't you just picture them careening down the slope?"

She laughed again, and he grinned, enjoying her more than he'd planned to.

"That kind of fun isn't just for little kids," he told her. "Come on."

"What?" She hung back, not sure.

"Take my hand. Trust me." And once she'd surrendered it to him, he began to slide down the hill with her beside him. She shrieked but came along, and they slid, going faster and faster, until they landed in a tangled heap at the bottom.

She lost her cap and her hair was full of snow, but she was laughing as he pulled her to her feet and wiped the wetness from her face.

"You can't do this in the city," he said, though she had no idea why he would bring something like that up.

"No," she responded candidly. "At least not in Los Angeles."

Their gazes met and for no other reason than the pure delight of the moment, they both laughed. He led her over to a fallen log where he brushed off the snow as best he could and flopped down. He made room for her and somehow ended up with his arm around her shoulders. Not that she could feel it through the padding. But it was nice, nonetheless. It made her feel accepted by him.

"Do you miss it?" she asked as she looked over the beautiful landscape before them.

"What? City life?"

She nodded.

"Sure. There are things I miss." He thought for a moment. "Good restaurants, the theater, the sense of purpose and excitement."

She nodded again. "I would miss all that," she said softly.

"But there are a lot of other things I don't miss," he told her, his voice more gruff, as though warning her not to question him about his reasons. "And on balance, I'll take life here."

"You prefer life in the country," she mused, eyes half-closed. "I guess that proves you're really a redneck at heart, just like I thought from the beginning."

He gave a grunt that turned into a chuckle. "I've been called a redskin before," he told her, "but never a redneck."

She turned to search his face. "Are you Native American?" she asked, knowing the answer from looking at him and from Sam's earlier words.

"Only part. My grandfather was Apache, so they tell me."

"You never knew him?"

"Nope."

She settled back beside him. "So *that's* where you got the name Lonewolf."

He hesitated. He wasn't used to opening up his personal life to anyone. But there was something comfortable about this woman, something that seemed to pry the secrets out of him. And he didn't even mind.

"Well, not quite," he told her slowly. "I don't really know what my grandfather's last name was. My father got the name Lonewolf in the orphanage where he grew up. Whether or not it came from the Apache, I don't know. That's what they called him, and it stuck."

She smiled. "It fits you."

He nodded. "It seems to," he admitted.

"So did you grow up on a reservation or anything like that?"

"No." He laughed shortly. "Not at all. I grew up in the city. I never knew much about my ancestral roots—not my father's Apache heritage, nor my mother's British and French background. I was just an American kid, like anyone else."

He looked down at her pretty mouth and had a twinge. Not used to talking so much about himself, he felt uneasy, and made a stab at changing the subject.

"How about you?" he said quickly. "How do you get to be a fern journal publisher, anyway?"

She made a face. This was never an elevating topic for her. "I majored in journalism in college," she said somewhat evasively.

"Oh. I see." He cocked a cynical eyebrow. "And then you graduated and decided, hey, what the world really needs is a fern journal."

She looked at him and laughed. It was amazing how much warmth his eyes could hold. Earlier this evening, she'd thought they were the coldest eyes she'd ever seen. But now...she felt warmed by his gaze, comforted by his arm, protected and at peace, and so she told him the truth, even though she had a feeling he would only half believe it.

"Nope. It wasn't quite that simple. First I spent a few years working on an underground newspaper." She made a face. "It was pretty awful. We specialized in four-letter words and illiterate rock groups."

He groaned and she grinned. "Yes, believe it or not. But that got old very quickly. You might say I finally grew up."

"And came above ground, to the ferns."

She rolled her eyes. "Very funny."

"Thank you."

She stared at him, shaking her head. That feeling was coming over her again, that urge to kiss him. She wanted to throw her arms around his neck and kiss him hard on the mouth, just for being him. With no idea why she was so strongly drawn to him, she just was, and she was enjoying it with all her heart.

"Actually, what happened was—my uncle had been publishing this fern journal since before I could remember. And he was ready to retire. So he offered it to me. I mean, I was the logical one to take it over, with my background in journalism."

"Not to mention the four-letter words." He grinned at her teasingly. "I'll bet that comes in handy."

She made a swat at him, and then a face. "You'd be surprised."

"And I suppose you were crazy about ferns."

"Actually, not. After writing interviews with groups like Spike My Headache and the Slugs and Nail Us to the Ground, I thought ferns would be pretty darn boring."

"But you were soon caught up in the romance of spores and filtered light."

"Not really. Not at first." Throwing back her head, she took in a huge gulp of icy air and reveled in it. "But you know, I am now. Ferns are really such neat, eerie plants. They're like dinosaurs, left over from an earlier age. And the more I got into them, the more I began to appreciate how unique they are. Now, I'm a real fernophile."

He shook his head, grinning to himself. No one could make that up. She *had* to be Cami Bishop. There was no longer a doubt in his mind.

So...what now? What was he going to do with her? He had her booked. He couldn't just let her go without something he could document that would exonerate her. And so far, he didn't have that. He only had his own gut feelings. Besides, there was no use in rushing things. He was going to have to go up and take a look at her car—make sure it hadn't been damaged in the storm and would still get her to Denver.

And then she would go, and she would be out of his life forever. But that was just as well. She had no place here. She was a passing breeze. And that, he decided firmly, was the way it had better stay.

"It is so beautiful," she said, and sighed. "How long have you lived here?"

"Almost three years," he said shortly. He didn't like to remember any further back than that.

She turned and scanned his face, curious. "Why did you choose this place to come to?"

Here we go, he was thinking. Why can't women ever leave good enough alone? They always asked too many questions. "They needed a sheriff right when I needed a job," he told her, trying for a short answer and looking away.

"Happy coincidence." She could see the evasiveness in his face, but that only made her more determined to dig for information. "But why here? It seems so different from Los Angeles."

"It is very different from Los Angeles. It's another world, another planet."

"What made you turn so strongly against the city?" she asked softly, treading carefully with her words, as she could see she was entering forbidden territory.

"A lot of things." He glanced at her and his eyes were dark and impassive again. "I got sick of the violence." Ordinarily this was where he would jump up and stride away, but for some reason, he looked into the depths of her eyes and found himself going on. "I got wind of this job and it seemed like the perfect antidote. Not only was it peaceful here, but the place is close to a number of reservations, Apache, Pueblo, Navaho. I thought it would be a good chance to learn something about my grandfather's people."

He could see that his answer pleased her, and for some stupid, strange reason, that pleased him. He looked away and tried to harden his heart, but it didn't work. Rising abruptly from the log, he reached to pull her to her feet.

"Let's get started back," he said gruffly. "It's going to take a lot longer going that way."

And it definitely did. Uphill in the snow was slow going. When she was completely out of breath and wilting with the effort, he swung her up into his arms and carried her.

"I'm too heavy," she protested, feeling awkward at first.

"No, you're not." And from the pace he set, without any visible signs of stress, she decided he was right.

So she settled back and enjoyed being carried through a winter wonderland by a big, strong man—a man whose breath smelled like the wind from the pines, whose arms felt hard and muscular, whose gaze sent her heartbeat racing. He set her down at the top of the hill and she turned back to look at their tracks in the snow. Spreading her arms, she took it all in.

"This place must be wonderful at Christmas," she said. "I'd love to come back here at that time of year." Turning, she smiled up at him. "Do you think you could arrange to have me arrested next year around the end of November?"

"Why not?" He wasn't smiling, but his eyes were warm again. "I'll have to have you extradited from California. Just be sure you do something to give me cause."

"Okay. Before I go, maybe I'll steal something. Something you won't notice until about next winter."

"Good idea." And for one simple second, he thought she might mean his heart, but then he squashed that thought. Much too sentimental, and if there was anything he couldn't stand, it was mushy, touchy-feely crap.

Besides, there was going to be none of that. He was having a good time with her, that he would have to admit. And he'd been carried away for a while there earlier in the night. But that was over now. He wasn't going to let that happen again.

"Let's get on back," he suggested, and they began the long trudge.

She walked along beside him, her boots crunching in the snow, as happy as she'd been in ages. It was like a wonderful winter dream. If only the dream didn't end with her behind bars. That did tend to kill the mood.

The room was warm and they shed their snow clothes by the heater. They joked as they undressed, but they avoided looking into each other's eyes. They both felt the awkwardness of not being sure what was going to happen next.

"I'll go back in the cell," she said as she hung up the last wet item to dry. "I'd better be in there before people begin arriving in the morning."

He gave her a narrow look. "What are you talking about?"

She waved away any objections he might have. "I understand how things like this work. I'm supposed to be locked in that cell. If the wrong person comes in and sees us... hobnobbing together, you could be in big trouble."

His gaze darkened and he thought fleetingly of all the other times he'd been on the wrong side of some rule or other. His run-ins with superiors had often been rough. But he'd always survived. "I can handle trouble."

She nodded thoughtfully. She was sure he could. "But I don't know if I can handle getting you into trouble," she noted. "Besides, I want to lie down. It's not light yet. Maybe I can get some sleep."

He moved restlessly, not sure what he wanted or what he wanted her to do. "Yeah, that's probably a good idea. And then, in the morning..."

She didn't want to think about the morning. Moving by quick instinct and on no other motive, she stood on her tiptoes and kissed him on the mouth. The kiss was quick and smooth, and as she drew back, she whispered, "Thanks for a magical night," then turned and made her way to her cell.

He watched her go, his heart beating wildly in his chest. Every part of him was urging that he follow her. But he wasn't going to do it. Not this time.

Six

Banks of snow were pillowed around the lovely pond. Hot springs bubbled beneath the surface, sending a cloak of fog to cloud the area. The woman turned, and Rafe squinted, trying to see her through the mist. At first, all he saw was a sheet of golden hair that floated about her face. Then his attention was diverted by her warm, round and very naked body. She was just coming out of the pond and drops of water sparkled everywhere, in her hair, on her skin. Her breasts were full, pink tipped and lovely. Her waist was small, her hips curved, protecting a triangle of spun gold. He ached for her even before her face was revealed through a parting in her thick hair and he knew it was Cami. He was going to have her this time. Moving in slow motion, he reached for her, reached and reached and . . . and suddenly the shimmering air turned dark and thunder clapped somewhere in the distance, and she was laughing and turning away from him, and just as his hand reached and almost touched her, she presented her back to him and his gaze dropped. There was a heart tattooed on her behind—a big, garish, electric-pink heart with a snake wrapped around it, like something a biker's woman would use for decoration. And when he looked up, she was looking back at him over her shoulder, and her face had changed. It wasn't Cami any longer. Not really. It was someone who looked like her but used heavy makeup and sneered and laughed at him mockingly.

"No," he was saying, backing away. "No, no..."

And then he was falling into a black hole and the next thing he knew, he was catching himself, about to tumble right out of his desk chair and onto the floor.

A dream. That was all it was. He shook his head to clear it, then looked into the cell to see if he'd woken Cami, but she was sound asleep, her cheek on her hand. She looked like an angel, and completely unlike the harpy who had appeared at the end of his dream.

But who was she really? How did he know for sure?

It occurred to him that all he had to do was walk over and push aside some cloth, and he would know. If she had a tattoo, was it anything like the tawdry one he'd imagined in his dream? He groaned, putting his head in his hands. He was becoming obsessed with this. He had to clear his mind.

But he couldn't get the dream to leave him alone. As he sat pondering it, going back over it again and again, he had to admit it had some use as a warning. Whether his subconscious mind had meant it that way or not, it was a reminder.

Things were not always as they seemed. He'd been in law enforcement long enough to know that was true. The very best criminals were often the very best actors. He no longer believed that Cami was Billie Joe. But he'd been wrong before. Hadn't he?

He'd been wrong about Janie at first. He'd thought she was weak and worthless to him as a partner. He'd been angry when she'd been paired with him. He'd even gone so far as to file a complaint.

But it hadn't taken long for Janie to make him eat his words. She'd done it with style and panache, but she'd never rubbed his nose in it. When she won him over, he fell all the way. All the way. And when she'd died at his side, taking a bullet that was probably meant for him, he'd lost everything that mattered in his life.

There'd been a hearing. There had been officers who'd accused him of being too close to his partner, of having his judgment blinded by the way he felt about her. He'd agonized over that for months, but he'd finally decided it hadn't really been a factor.

Still, he had to consider the possibility that he was letting his emotions get in the way again. Did his feelings cloud his discretion? Was he letting Cami's natural attractions affect his view of things?

There was no doubt he was attracted. He could barely hold back the compulsion to go to her right now. It was a fascination very different from what he'd had with Janie. That had been love, and a deep affection based on mutual respect. This was... this was... What the hell was this?

Insanity. That might be the best word for it. Every time he looked at her, his insides churned. She scared him. And that was exactly why he was going to keep control. He couldn't let things get out of hand, as they almost had a few hours before. He couldn't let it happen.

He glanced at his briefcase. Janie's picture was in there. He should pull it out, prop it up and make a signal to all the world that here was where his heart lay. Here, and nowhere else.

But he didn't do it. An invisible hand seemed to be holding him back. So he sat very still in his chair, and he slowly fell asleep again. And this time he didn't dream at all.

*　*　*

Morning was heralded by the arrival of a delegation of the area children at the door. Rafe woke up with a jolt when they knocked. Frowning, he stumbled groggily to open up, flinching as a blast of cold air greeted him, and there on his doorstep stood three young boys, each bundled up in a heavy jacket, scarf and boots, none of them older than twelve.

"Hi, kids," he said, rubbing his eyes and looking out at the peaceful sight of newly fallen snow covering everything. But dawn had barely broken. It was still pretty early and the sky had barely changed from purple to gold and blue. He looked down at the children and frowned. "What can I do for you?"

The tallest gazed up at him, his round face earnest. "We came to see the lady that's in your jail," he said.

Rafe's eyes opened all the way. "You did, huh?" He turned and looked at where Cami still lay dozing on the cot, the covers pulled up, completely decorous. Looking back down at the children, his brows drew together. "Who told you I had a lady in my jail?" he asked gruffly.

The tallest took a deep breath. "Jimmy said he heard Chief White Horse tell Andy Cruz that Mrs. Cricket called up Angie Andrews and told her that Beatrice was at the Laundromat last night and she said that Sheriff Lonewolf had a lady..."

"Okay." Rafe held up a hand to stop the endless sentence from rolling out and drowning them all. "Okay, okay." He looked at their faces. Expectation was hidden behind dark eyes that gazed out from beneath straight-cut black hair, but it was there. He glanced at Cami again. She seemed sound asleep. What the heck. Who would it hurt?

"Well, all right," he told the children softly. "But come in quietly. Take a look, and then get on out of here. Okay?"

They nodded, their dark eyes bright with anticipation. Filing in, oldest to youngest, they made their way across the room and stood silently a few feet away from the bars.

No one spoke for a long moment, and then the smallest whispered loudly, "What's she doin' in there?"

She stirred and Rafe winced. "She *was* sleeping."

The youngest turned and looked up at him. "Her eyes are open," he noted.

Rafe nodded sadly. "They are now," he murmured. His gaze met Cami's sleepy eyes and he tried a smile. "Good morning," he mouthed silently, but she didn't respond. And, he noticed, she didn't smile, either.

He could hardly blame her. Who wanted to wake up and find a group of kids watching you like a museum display? It was time he herded them on out and he lifted his arms to do just that, but before he could tell them it was time to go, the tallest piped up with a new observation.

"I remember when Harry Moon was in here," he said. "That time he dropped acid."

They all nodded solemnly, their dark eyes huge. It was evidently a shared icon of their childhood experience, a touchstone, never to be forgotten.

"He wasn't like her," the smallest said, gesturing toward where Cami still lay on the cot.

"No. He looked sick. And he was snoring."

Cami sighed, shaking her head, but the children hardly noticed.

"And when he woke up," the smallest one said, remembering, "he looked kind of dumb."

"She doesn't look like that."

"No."

"She looks pretty."

Giving in to the inevitable, Cami sat up and gazed at them. "Thank you," she said.

They jumped backward, eyes wide, as though they hadn't realized she could hear them, much less that she might talk back.

"She said something," one whispered to another.

"Was she talking to us?"

They came back, moving carefully, and stood close to the bars.

"Hey, lady. Why are you in there?" the tallest called to her, as though she were somehow farther away than the four or five feet that stood between them.

Cami yawned and smiled at them all sleepily. "That's a very good question. Maybe you'd better ask the sheriff." She aimed a complacent smile his way. "He's the one who put me here."

The three of them turned and stared at the sheriff. He hesitated. His first impulse was to order them out the door, but his better nature intervened. After all, he was a figure of authority in this tiny town, and as such, he had a responsibility to help raise the children. Perhaps it was time a few of them learned about how these things worked.

Sighing, he sank to sit on the corner of his desk and gestured for the children to join him. "Okay, gather 'round now. I'll tell you all about it."

They moved quickly, forming a circle around him as though he were the town storyteller, staring up eagerly into his face.

"You see, I got news of a warrant for the arrest of a..." He hesitated, glancing at Cami, who was looking on with interest. "Of a woman who was wanted by the police in a couple of states. This warrant was for a lady who was from out of town."

"A stranger?"

"That's right. They said she was blond, very pretty, about thirty years old. Does that seem to apply to anyone you could think of?"

Each pair of dark eyes turned and stared at Cami. She smiled back. There didn't seem to be anything else to do.

"Okay. This blond lady was supposed to be driving a green Mustang. And guess what kind of car our guest was driving when I found her."

They looked from him to Cami and back again, not saying a word.

"A green Mustang," he supplied for them. "She was driving it up on the old forest road."

"That road's closed," the smallest chirped.

He nodded. "You're right. And that was another reason I had to suspect her."

The youngster's tiny dark face contorted as he squinted, trying to understand it all. "So she got arrested 'cuz she was driving on the old forest road?"

"No," he said patiently. "I arrested her because all the items fit the warrant. And just her being on a closed road was suspicious. She might have been trying to find a place to hide."

They stared at him and no one said a word. He frowned. Something told him they were not convinced.

"Don't you see? I thought she might be the person in the warrant." His frown deepened. "I had to hold her, just to make sure."

The smallest looked at Cami again. "What's her name?" he asked.

That was a good question. Rafe looked at her and she responded for him.

"My name's Cami Bishop," she told the children. "The sheriff thinks I'm someone named Billie Joe Calloway. She's a person who's done some bad things."

The little one looked stricken. "You don't look like a bad lady," he said softly, biting his lower lip as he gazed at her.

"You're right," she told him firmly. "I'm not that bad lady. She's someone else."

They swung around to confront Rafe.

"She's not the bad lady. Why don't you let her go?"

Rafe groaned internally, but he had to maintain a firm, strong image for the children, so he didn't let them see how uncomfortable he was with this question.

"Sometimes you have to hold on to people until you get better information. It's like..." He thought for a moment. "Okay, it's like this. Say you have a new puppy, and your neighbor says he saw a dog that looks just like yours digging up his tomato plant. He gives you a description, and you could swear it has to be your new puppy. You never saw your puppy do anything like that, and you find it hard to believe. It makes you sad to think your puppy is in so much trouble, but you keep him in the house all day, just in case."

"Then you find out your neighbor is lying?" guessed the tallest.

"No, not exactly..."

"Then you find out there's another puppy just like yours." The middle child nodded, confident he had it right. "And maybe he's the one who did it."

"That's it," Rafe said, pointing at the middle child and nodding, as well. "That's exactly what I mean."

"So you are waiting to find out that there's another lady around here that looks like this lady?" the tallest asked, skeptical.

"Sort of."

"So she's like a prisoner," said the middle child with relish, eyes sparkling.

Rafe winced. "Sort of," he admitted. "But..."

"A prisoner!" They didn't need to hear any more. They liked that. All three turned and looked at her, eyes wide. "A prisoner!"

"Let's go tell the other kids," the tallest suggested, and the three of them were out the door and up the street in no time.

Rafe turned a sheepish glance toward Cami. She raised an eyebrow and said, musingly, "I knew if I played my cards right I'd be famous someday."

She wasn't really angry. She was too busy marveling at him to be angry. He looked even better this morning with the early sun streaming in and filling his face with gold than he had the night before in lamplight. Why couldn't she have found a man like this down in Los Angeles? Were all the good ones hiding in the hills somewhere?

"Uh...sorry about that," he said, still looking a bit baleful. "I thought I could let them come in and take a peek and be out before you woke up."

"Oh, that's all right," she said airily. "It isn't every day I get compared to a new puppy."

But she was smiling. It was funny, really. She enjoyed the way he'd related to the children. That was something of a surprise, actually. Who would have guessed this big, gruff man would be a cream puff around short people?

She spent some time in the bathroom, freshening up, and while she was in there, Sam came in with her breakfast. He was setting it up in the cell when she came out, and Rafe was nowhere to be seen.

"Look here," Sam called to her cheerfully. "Pancakes and sausages. And I brought you tea *and* coffee. That mud Rafe makes in his machine isn't fit for a nice lady like you."

"Well, thank you, sir," she said, taking in the aroma of it all. "I'm starved."

Before she could sit down to enjoy her meal, a rumble began outside—a clattering, metallic noise that got louder and louder, shaking the earth. Startled, she turned to Sam. "What on earth is that?" she asked, clutching his sleeve.

He gazed down at her, amused. "Haven't you heard a snowplow before?"

She shook her head. "I'm from Southern California, remember?" Releasing him, she went to the window to watch the tractorlike machine as it rumbled past. "Does this mean the roads are open?"

Sam nodded. "Yup. The main highway, at any rate. They usually get to them pretty fast." Heaving a piteous sigh, he thumped his chest. "But I'm going up where no plow will go for hours."

She turned a questioning look his way. "Where is that?"

"The old forest road." He grinned at her. "I'm going up to see if I can find that purse Rafe tells me you dropped there last night. Got any idea on landmarks for me? I don't want to have to dig up all the snow along that road if I can help it."

Quickly she sketched in the best of her memory of the area. "Where's the sheriff?" she asked casually when she was finished.

"He went home to pick up a few things and see how his place weathered the storm." His eyes shone with unreleased laughter. "And he probably needed a little decompression time. You know what I mean?"

She ignored his friendly dig. "We've already had a visit from a group of children this morning," she told him. "They were really cute. How many people live in this town?"

"Oh, about five hundred, I guess. All sorts—farmers, ranchers, storekeepers, retired folks, young return-to-the-simple-life professionals. And we have a good ethnic blend, too. Being this close to three big reservations, we've got Pueblo families, Navaho families and even a few renegade Apaches, like old Rafe. Then we've got descendants of pioneers from over a hundred years ago, Irish and English and Swedes. An Italian family moved in about ten years ago. And there are people of Mexican background scattered all through the mix."

"A little United Nations," she murmured.

"Hey, we're all Americans," he reminded her. "And as such, we get along a lot better than those countries do at the UN."

She laughed. "I'm glad to hear that."

Before she could ask him anything else, Rafe came in through the doorway. He looked at Sam suspiciously.

"Has he been gabbing your ear off?" he asked her as he made his way toward his desk, his gaze darting from one of them to the other, as though he were wary of what Sam might have been telling her. "Some Navaho," he grumbled as he stowed a few things into his drawer.

Sam's good-natured laugh boomed out as he headed for the doorway. "I'll get that purse for you, lady," he called back. "Be back soon." And he disappeared, slamming the door behind him.

Cami sauntered slowly into the cell and sat down to begin her breakfast, but at the same time, she watched Rafe as he involved himself in busywork, then asked him curiously, "Why do you always comment on how much Sam talks?"

Rafe looked up at her, his face hard, as though he were steeling himself for something. But as he looked at her, he softened somehow, and then he shook his head, as though giving in to something and half laughing at himself about it.

"Why do I comment on Sam all the time?" he repeated, looking toward her but not actually meeting her gaze. "Because he's a Navaho. That's why."

She shrugged, fascinated by the struggle she'd just witnessed in his face, wanting to keep him talking. "So?" she prodded.

"Don't you know about the Navaho?" Reluctantly his gaze met hers. "They're known as a quiet people. They don't usually talk unless they've really got something to say, and then only when invited to give their opinion." His mouth twisted as he thought of an example. "Take Jake Waterhorn. He'll come by and sit outside, waiting to be invited in. He doesn't want to bother us, so he waits until we notice him and ask him in. Then he comes in here and sits down and waits for us to begin the conversation. Most Navaho are like that. They don't intrude.''

Bemused, she shook her head. "Are they shy?''

"Not at all. They just have their own rhythm. They're a unique bunch. A quiet, contemplative people.''

"That doesn't sound much like Sam.'' Remembering how the big man had come through the room like a noisy tornado, she smiled.

Rafe felt more of his interior ice melt every time she did that. He knew how she was affecting him, and he didn't seem to be able to stop it. What worried him most was the feeling that he didn't want to stop it.

"That's exactly the point,'' he told her, shaking away his thoughts. "He's the exception that proves the rule.'' And then, just because he couldn't help it, an irrepressible grin lit his face. "I love the guy. He's the best deputy I could have up here. But he never stops talking.''

She definitely liked the grin. She only wished she knew how to make him hand out more of them. Sighing, she went back to eating her breakfast. It was delicious and she found she was very hungry. But all the time, she was watching Rafe, thinking about him. She had to admit it—she was liking this man more and more. First the way he was with the children, now the way he unselfconsciously declared his feelings for his deputy—she was drawn to him. But there were still things she had to know.

"Do you have any kids of your own?'' she asked without thinking, rising from the cot and leaving the rest of her breakfast behind her.

He looked up from the paperwork, startled. "No, of course not. I've never been married.''

"Oh.'' She came toward him, then stood gazing at him, her head to the side. She'd thought that was the way it was, but she'd wanted it confirmed. "You're good with kids,'' she told him. "You'll make a good father someday.''

Shrugging, he turned away. He wasn't about to get into a discussion of how unlikely that prospect was. Avoiding her gaze, he pulled out more papers and a new pen and began some mindless paperwork that still needed to be done.

She sank into the chair across the desk from where he was sitting. Didn't he realize what she'd said was a compliment? It didn't seem that he did.

"When do I get released?" she asked, prodding him.

He looked up quickly, then narrowed his eyes. "Who says you're getting released?" he asked. Snapping back his cuff, he took a look at his watch. "In another hour I'll make the call to Santa Fe and we'll see if we can get this straightened out," he said. "Until then, you're stuck here."

She sighed, leaning back in the chair. He'd replaced the protective shield and he had that look again, that *I don't need a woman in my life so don't bother me* look—a look she was rapidly learning to resent. "If the phones are back, maybe I should make that phone call now."

"Sure." He picked up the phone and placed it in front of her. "Go right ahead."

His face was impassive. Not an emotion showed in his deep, dark eyes. So he really didn't care at all, she decided. It was all the same to him whom she called and what she did. There was a strange emotion building in her and she wasn't sure just what it was. But she did know he was annoying her.

"Why do you pretend you don't like kids?" she asked abruptly, ignoring the phone and frowning at him. "Nobody believes it."

There. She actually saw a tiny flare of something in his eyes. A feeling of satisfaction sizzled through her. He *could* be reached if you tried hard enough.

He didn't crack much, but he did throw down his pen, and it looked as though he were giving up the evasive action for the moment. "How do you know what people believe about me?" he returned calmly, sitting back to stare at her.

"It's obvious," she bluffed. "You think you're hiding it, but it shows."

He held her gaze for a long moment, and then the corners of his mouth began to curl and he shook his head, giving an exasperated laugh. "I don't even know what you're talking about," he protested. "What is going on here?"

"We're having a conversation," she said happily. "Can't you tell?"

"No." He shook his head again, then jabbed a forefinger in the air at her. "And I think you're the one with a problem about children. You're the one who's fixated on the subject."

She nodded. "You're right, but at least I admit it."

So that was it. He let his gaze run over her for a moment, but his mind was shuffling data and coming up with a conclusion. He could remember Janie using ploys like this. Cami wanted to talk, didn't she? She wanted him to put aside the paperwork and pay some attention to her.

Women were funny. They seemed to need this sort of communication the way vampires needed a nightly dose of blood—they became very fretful without it. He'd learned with Janie, it was best to let them have a taste of it periodically. That way they seemed much happier.

"Okay," he said agreeably, lacing his fingers together on the desk in front of him. "Go ahead. Tell me about you and kids."

She hesitated. "We're talking about you and kids," she reminded him. "Why do you try to pretend you don't care about them? They obviously adore you."

"They don't adore me. They look up to me. I'm the sheriff."

She nodded. "That's part of it. But you have a natural knack with kids. Now why would you want to deny it?" She fixed him with a steady gaze. "Haven't you ever considered having kids?"

His mouth tightened. "When you've seen the underside of life like I have," he said gruffly, "you wonder about bringing a kid into the world today. A kid that you love and want to protect." He winced, as though the very idea pained him. "Having kids is asking for heartbreak," he said quickly, then looked embarrassed by his own display of emotion.

She took a deep breath and let it out slowly. "That's life," she said, shaking her head. "It's always a gamble. But you don't get anything at all if you don't live it."

"I'll choose my gambles, thank you," he said dryly. "So how about you? You planning to have kids?"

She hesitated. That was a loaded question in her case. "I've always wanted kids," she admitted.

He nodded. "I sort of figured that out on my own," he drawled.

"And now here I am, going to a baby shower for my college roommate and best friend—"

"And feeling rotten about it."

"Yes." She realized, suddenly, how perceptive he really was. "Yes. And hating myself for feeling that way."

He nodded. "So quit feeling that way," he murmured, knowing that was the male approach, the quick fix that no woman worth her salt would give a second thought.

"I can't quit what I'm feeling," she said. "But you see, that's what's so...hard about this. I was the one who always wanted a family." Her eyes focused on the far wall as she remembered. "In college, they used to make fun of me. I was the old-fashioned one, aiming at being a housewife, while the others all had high-flying careers in mind. And now..." She paused and consciously lowered her voice. "And now Sara is having a baby. And it looks like I probably won't."

Ordinarily he would be discomfited by a disclosure like this. He didn't go in for confessions. But there was something about her, something about her air of innocent faith, that touched him. And he was pleased that she'd thought she could tell him about something that was obviously so intimate—and so painful. He only wished he had the slightest clue as to what he could say or do that would make her feel better. "You'll have a baby someday," he said awkwardly, trying to be reassuring.

She shook her head. She'd just about given up hope of that.

He made a futile gesture and looked away. "There are a lot of guys out there," he muttered.

"I know." She gazed out the window at the sun on the new snow. "I've dated most of them." She shook her head. "But the right one isn't out there. If he was, I would have found him by now. I've certainly done my share of looking." She tried a tremulous smile. "For a few years there I went through more boyfriends than Mae West." She shook her head and went on in a determinedly cheerful voice. "They say all the good guys are already married. So maybe that's why I couldn't find one of them out there single and running free."

"They say a lot of things that aren't true," he reminded her, wishing he could think of something clever to say, feeling impotent.

But she really didn't need comfort. She just needed to talk. "A couple of years ago, I pretty much gave up. I actually looked into doing it on my own—adoption, insemination, sperm banks, and all that."

The entire idea was horrifying to him, but he tried to hide it. "What stopped you?"

She turned her palms up and smiled. "Once I stared reality in the face, I realized it wouldn't be fair to the baby to make it grow up without a father. I mean, I would be satisfying my own selfish desires at the expense of the child. And I truly feel that, once you make the commitment to have a child, the welfare of that child has to come first until it's raised."

He searched her eyes, trying to see behind the words, trying to see into her heart. The decision she'd made was a painful one, but she'd made it with courage and a generosity of spirit that you didn't often see. He had to admit, he was impressed.

"So you're still looking for a man to help you make a family." He stated it flatly, as though it were a view he couldn't completely understand.

"I suppose you could say that," she said slowly.

He stared at her for a long moment, seeing something there that made him wary. All this empathy was well and good, as long as it didn't lead to an intimacy he couldn't afford to risk. Hardening his heart, he shrugged and turned his shoulder toward her.

"Well, don't look at me," he warned, trying to make it sound lighthearted, but coming out cold and hard instead.

His quick snap was like a splash of cold water in her face, and she reacted in kind. Here she'd been opening up her soul to this man, and now he was going to get flippant? "Who in the world said anything about looking at you?" she demanded, her anger flaring quickly. "I can't believe you said that!"

Wrong move. He could see that now. He tried to salvage the situation. "I didn't mean to—"

"Oh, I see. You didn't mean to warn me off. Spoke too soon, did you?" But she was hurt. Here she'd felt they were getting along so well, and then he said something that negated all the closeness between them. Of all the—

"I mean, what are you to me, anyway? Only the man who grabbed me out of my car while I was on my way to a baby shower, arrested me for something I didn't do, for being someone I'm not, plunked me down in jail, put me through the humiliation of a body search . . ."

"Body search?" Now she was going too far. After all, he'd gone out of his way to avoid humiliating her in that search. And this was the thanks he got? "I did no such thing. Though I should have."

Her chin jutted out and her eyes flashed. "You tried. I wouldn't let you."

His mouth twisted in a macho sneer. "Listen, 'letting' me had nothing to do with it."

"Oh, yeah?" Jumping up, she whirled in front of him. "Big talk, Mr. Sheriff. I'm still untouched. You wouldn't dare lay a hand on me now."

"Is that a challenge?" He rose and faced her, jutting jaw to jutting jaw. "Are you daring me?" he demanded, his eyes hot with his own anger.

"Oh, you'd love an excuse to lock me up, wouldn't you?"

He didn't need an excuse. Didn't she get it? He'd arrested her, damn it! And he was being darn nice letting her wander around the office this way, instead of keeping her behind bars. He wanted to shake her, but an idea flashed into his mind instead.

"Okay. Here's a challenge for you," he said with some disdain. "Prove to me that you aren't Billie Joe Calloway. Show me—right here—right now—that you don't have the tattoo."

She blanched. "What?" she said, her voice rather higher than it had been.

Aha. His eyes lit with gratification. Now he had her. "Come on," he taunted. "If you're so brave. I want to see it."

She felt light-headed, but she wasn't about to let him sense weakness in her, so she didn't try to sit down. Instead, she shifted her weight from foot to foot and chewed on her lower lip. "There are a lot of things you may want in this world, mister. That doesn't mean you're going to get them."

He straightened and looked down his hawklike nose at her. "You can settle this right now. All you have to do is show me."

She blinked at him, breathless. "You still think I'm Billie Joe?" she asked, aghast.

He stared at her for a moment, then shook his head slowly. "No, I don't think you're Billie Joe. I can't believe you could possibly be Billie Joe." He thumped on his chest. "But I'm still a cop. And I need the proof. And much as I don't think you are, I still think you could be."

She frowned. "That's the same thing," she said accusingly.

"No, it's not the same thing at all." Triumph lit his gaze. "And you're trying to change the subject. Because you're chicken."

She flushed. He had her there. But she couldn't admit it. "Am not," she said stubbornly.

"Are too," he said right back. "I dared you. And you backed down."

"Well . . . well, *I* dare *you!*"

His eyes glinted with satisfaction. She'd given up. "To do what?"

"To . . . to . . ."

Suddenly she was closer and her hands were on his chest, as though she might push him away, but her face was turned up toward his, and her lips were parted. It happened so quickly, and he hadn't seen it coming at all. Her blue eyes met his dark ones, and there was a mist in their depths, a sense of alluring mystery that drew him closer.

"I dare you to quit pretending you don't want to kiss me," she whispered.

He didn't know how this could happen when he'd been so dead set against it. They'd been fighting, for Pete's sake. He'd just won the argument, and then, all of a sudden, he was doing exactly what he'd sworn he wouldn't do again.

But when she was this close, and the scent of her hair filled him with memories of springtime, and the touch of her hands sent his pulse skyrocketing, and her mouth was so close, so tempting . . .

And then her mouth was under his, yielding to him, and his hands were on her, sliding up beneath her silk blouse, spanning her back as though he could take possession of her if he wanted to.

There were no words for what this felt like. It almost didn't feel. It just was. There was heat involved, lots of heat. And a light, sinking sensation, as though he were being drawn into something plush and soft and smooth, as though he were drowning, but he didn't care. And then there was that surge in his body, that feeling of urgent need, that impulse to bend her back and find his way between her legs…

But right now something else was happening. He was going to have to come up for air, swim his way through the heat and find a way to breathe, or he wasn't going to last much longer.

They came apart with a gasp, but his arms were holding her tightly, so tightly there was no fear he would be letting go. She took in gulps of air, regaining her balance. Looking into his dark eyes, she laughed softly.

"I couldn't breathe," she told him, gazing at him in wonder.

"Neither could I," he admitted, looking down at her pretty face, wanting to devour every bit of her, take her all in and hold her for his own—forever.

"It's okay," she whispered, reaching for him again. "I don't really need to breathe."

His face felt rough and it was a delicious friction against her skin. She pressed her body to his, wanting to feel all of his hardness, his angles and barriers, wanting to mold her softness to him everywhere. She had never known this before—this sense of losing herself in a man. His mouth was hard and hot and delicious and she never wanted to taste anything else but him again.

I could love this man, her mind was telling her. *Go ahead. Let your heart open to him. Be free. Because you could love him.*

"Yes," she murmured, wrapping her arms around his neck. "Oh, yes."

No, he was thinking, gathering all his strength to try to turn away from her lovely face, her luscious body. No, this wasn't right. He couldn't do this. In his groggy state of mind, it was hard to remember just why it was that this was not allowed to him, but he knew it wasn't. And he had to pull away before things went too far.

"Hold on," he said huskily, raising his face from hers.

She gazed up at him as though seeing him through a fog. "Rafe," she murmured, reaching to pull him back.

"No." He drew away roughly, catching her by the shoulders. "We can't do this," he said sternly, waking her up to reality. "I'm the cop. You're the prisoner. Remember? This is wrong."

Wrong? How could it be wrong? She shook her head, trying to clear it. "But I'm not Billie Joe," she said huskily. "So it doesn't matter."

She reached for him and he groaned, closing his eyes as her hands framed his face, caressing him, drawing him back.

A sound at the door shattered the moment. She turned, and so did Rafe, parting quickly. The front door had opened a crack, and for some reason, probably having just a little to do with guilt, Cami retreated to the cell, as though afraid someone might object to the sight of the prisoner running free. And at the same time, she scolded herself. But she relaxed when the door opened a little wider and a small parade of youngsters began filing into the building. They moved too quickly to count, but she could see that there were six or eight of them.

"Hey, kids," Rafe said, trying to head them off at the pass, a move that failed when he didn't make it quickly enough. "Whoa, stop right there. This isn't a zoo. You can't just come in and gawk anytime you feel like it."

The little girl in the lead paid no attention. Her gaze was full on Cami. She stopped a few feet away from her and stared, eyes wide.

Rafe gritted his teeth, looking at the group and shaking his head.

"Okay, you want to see the prisoner, don't you? Well, take a look, and then get on out of here. The lady has rights, too, you know, and she doesn't like being stared at...."

But they weren't listening. Their eyes were huge as they surveyed this wonder in their very own local jail cell.

The little dark-haired girl who seemed to be the leader of the group was the first to speak. "Jeremy Pierce, take a look," she said, pulling a younger boy up to the front row to see better. "She's got yellow hair, just like your mom. Has your mom ever been in jail like this?"

"Nope," said Jeremy stoutly. "But she did get a ticket for speeding once, down in Santa Fe. I was with her." Jeremy puffed out his chest and the others looked at him enviously for a moment, mulling over the glory of it all.

"My mom never gets arrested or nothin'," the smallest said in disgust.

"Okay," Rafe said sternly, beginning to herd them out again. "Show's over."

The little girl turned to leave reluctantly, then stopped and pulled on Rafe's sleeve, asking, "Sheriff Lonewolf. How come you keep her here like this? How come?"

"Yeah," the others chimed in, the back ones jumping up and down to better see him. "How come?"

The little girl narrowed her eyes dramatically. "Is she dangerous?"

Rafe considered this for a moment, gazing at Cami. "Yup," he told them at last. "She's very dangerous. I have to watch my step around her."

A visceral thrill ran through the little group. "What'll she do to you? Huh? What?"

His mouth twisted and he glanced at Cami, his eyes smoldering with laughter, before quickly looking away. "Never mind that," he told the kids. "Get on out, now."

"Are you going to keep her here all spring?" the girl asked as they shuffled toward the door.

Rafe shrugged and said with a perfectly straight face, "Maybe. If I feel like it."

Their little mouths gaped at him. This was better than the snowstorm.

"Now you all go on home," he told them firmly. "The lady needs to get some rest."

They shuffled toward the door, looking back over their shoulders, and when they got out in the snow, one of them yelled to a passing car, "Hey, guess what? We got to see Sheriff Lonewolf's lady."

Rafe groaned, and Cami shook her head. He turned and met her gaze, looking sheepish.

"Well, you've had your fun," she said, suppressing her own laughter. "Now, if you're finished terrorizing the kids of this town, I'm going to sit my dangerous self down and finish this breakfast."

"Sorry," he said gruffly. "But it was only the truth."

She stared at him for a moment. He wasn't smiling. He was dead serious.

"Go on," he said softly. "You'd better eat before it all gets cold." He started to turn away, then looked back. "And don't take anything too seriously, Cami," he said. "Just remember that." And he returned to his work.

Cami. He'd said her name. It was the first time, and that fact in itself gave her a glow. She wanted him to touch her cheek, to drop a kiss on her mouth, but she could tell the moment was over, and it wasn't going to happen. Not right now.

"Okay," she said, drawing back. His eyes were dark, but they weren't hard or cold. She turned slowly, sighing as she went back to sit on her cot. But she was hugging a new secret close to her chest. She could fall in love with this man with very little effort. Should she let herself do it? Did she have any choice in the matter?

She devoured the rest of her breakfast and downed both the tea and the coffee, feeling warm and happy. Rafe was busy working, busy pretending he'd forgotten she existed, but that was okay. She'd felt the passion in his kiss, felt the need in his body. They weren't finished with each other yet. And it was almost time to call Santa Fe.

Seven

It wasn't long after that Sam was back. "Guess what I found," he said, waving the item as he came through the door.

"My purse!" Cami cried, reaching for it happily.

"Her purse," Sam said pointedly to Rafe.

"I get the general idea," Rafe said sardonically.

"Yes. And here is my identification." She dug into the purse and pulled out her little leather folder with her license and credit cards, thrusting them at him with an air of triumph. "Now, what more do you want?"

He took the folder from her and looked it over, but his face was impassive once again. Why wasn't he happier to know the truth? She didn't quite understand it. She wanted some happiness here. Did he want her to be guilty?

It was probably some police thing she didn't fully understand. She turned away restlessly, and her hand went to her hair. She was probably a mess. She hadn't really looked in a mirror yet today, and suddenly she was self-conscious about it.

"Tell you what," she suggested, pulling her tiny makeup case out of a side pocket. "Let me have my supplies, and my comb. You go ahead and peruse the contents of my purse. I'm going to freshen up a bit."

He nodded without speaking, but he watched her as she left the room, and she felt his gaze as though it burned into her back. At the exit, she glanced back. She met his eyes for a long moment, then went on into the little room.

Rafe sat staring at the closed door for a long time. Here was her purse, sitting right in front of him, and it was going to give plenty of evidence that she was exactly who she said she was. He knew that without even looking. And once he'd admitted it, what was he going to do? Let her go? If she wasn't Billie Joe, he had no right to hold her any longer. And if he didn't have a good reason to keep her here, she would be gone like a shot from a rifle. And if she left, he would never see her again.

No big deal. Who was she to him, anyway? Nobody. A tourist, passing through. A transitory amusement. It would be just as well if she went on her way.

But at the same time those thoughts were rolling through his head, he heard himself saying to Sam, "I'm going to have to take her on down to Santa Fe to clear this whole thing up."

Sam, uncharacteristically silent, merely stared at him.

"I've got to be sure," Rafe persisted, trying to keep the defensive tone out of his voice. "They have female wardens down there. And the fingerprints. And the mug shots. We can check this thing out and get it settled."

Sam still didn't comment, and Rafe rose and went to the television, turning on the morning news, hoping to drown out his own thoughts at this point. Then he went to the telephone and dialed, prepared to make plans. He knew what he proposed to do would add another six to ten hours to the time he would have to put up with Cami and her complaints. Oh, well. There were just some sacrifices he had to make for law enforcement, and this was one of them. He didn't feel good about it. But somehow, he did feel as though he had no other choice.

Cami was hurrying through her makeup routine, humming a theme from a romantic movie as she worked. A little lip gloss, a little eyeliner, and she was back in business, feeling more human. For some reason, her heart was light as a feather. She couldn't imagine why. But she gave herself a big grin in the mirror, straightened her blouse and turned to rejoin the men.

She opened the door quietly and looked out. Both men had their backs to her. Sam was lounging in front of the television, and Rafe was on the telephone. She smiled. Surely he was calling Santa Fe. Coming up softly behind him, she listened to what he was saying into the receiver.

"...I'd appreciate it if he could get the paperwork ready."

Yes, her arrest was coming to an end. She'd known he would see the light once he'd looked into her wallet.

"...yes, that's right. Billie Joe Calloway."

A wave of affection for him swept over her. When he turned around, she was going to ignore Sam's presence and ...

"I'm bringing her in for a positive ID. We ought to get to Santa Fe about noon...."

The truth hit her like a thunderbolt and shock stopped the breath in her throat. He wasn't convinced at all. He was taking her in. How could this be happening?

Stunned, she waited for him to get off the phone and explain himself. But when he replaced the receiver, he turned the other way, toward the file cabinet, and in a moment, he was noisily pulling out drawers, searching for something, his face relaxed—happy, even.

She'd never been so hurt, so angry in her life. Her body shook with it. They'd been so close, and she'd thought he believed her, thought he understood. Her first instinct was to confront him about it, but she quickly and angrily rejected that. Why should she? She'd been arguing with him all night and hadn't won an argument yet.

Her purse was sitting out on the desk, and someone had left the front door ajar. She grabbed her linen jacket and her fingers curled around the handle of her purse. Neither of them was paying her any attention. Tossing her curls back, she flounced out, knowing she wouldn't get very far, but determined to show him how angry she was.

Her shoes crunched on the snow and she slipped, but she got her balance back and kept going, walking angrily down the road. Where was she going? She didn't know. She was sure he would stop her any second, so it hardly mattered. She could almost feel him behind her, and she stopped, whirling to confront him. But it was only a dog, crossing the street as though he had something very important to take care of on the other side. She looked back at the sheriff's station. There wasn't a sign that they'd noticed her gone yet.

Well, that was just great. Angrier than ever, she turned back and surveyed her options. Anger was keeping her warm at the moment, but she knew that wouldn't last long without a coat. She was going to have to get somewhere heated, fast. She could stop in at one of the few houses along the side. Or she could hitchhike. But there hadn't been much traffic, and…her gaze fell on a sight that stopped her. Wasn't that the tail end of a bus? She walked a little more quickly. Sure enough, there was a bus stop in front of the country store, and a big, diesel-belching Greyhound stood there with its engine running.

As she approached, the driver came out of the store with a steaming cup of coffee in his hand.

"Where are you going?" she called out to him.

He looked at her and shrugged. "Bodine, the next town, for starters," he said good-naturedly. "And Denver is our ultimate goal."

"Oh." She glanced back at the silent landscape behind her. "Do you have an empty seat? Can I buy a ticket?"

"Sure. We've got plenty of room." He gestured for her to get on board. "Go ahead and get on. I'll have your ticket ready by the next stop. I want to get going, because with this new snow, I'm already running late."

"Great."

She climbed aboard and headed for a seat in the back. The bus began to move and she looked out the back window, watching the sheriff's station retreat into the distance. As it got smaller and smaller, her heart beat faster and faster. What was she doing? This was almost like...why, you would have to call this— "Oh, my God. I've just made a jailbreak," she whispered to herself, horrified. Unbelievable. And it had been so easy.

Rafe looked up from where he'd slumped into a chair next to Sam to watch the rest of the news. Pulling back his cuff, he glanced at his watch. "How long's she going to be in there?" he grumbled.

Sam switched off the television and turned, looking around the room. "You know women," he murmured. "So, what do you want to do about her car?"

"It's still up on the old forest road, and so's the snow."

"I know. I've just been up there. Remember?"

Rafe hesitated. "I guess we could leave it for now. With the sun shining this hard, we'll get a lot of melting this afternoon. We could probably go up before dusk and get it out."

"Think you'll be back from Santa Fe by then?"

Rafe turned away, not wanting Sam to see what he was afraid might be showing in his eyes. "Maybe. Depends on how quickly we get through the forms. Who knows?" He risked a quick glance at his deputy. "We may have to stay the night down there."

"Yeah," Sam said, forcing back the smile that threatened. "That would be a real shame."

"Yeah."

The two men tried hard not to let their gazes meet, but when they finally did, they both grinned.

"Shut up," Rafe said, swearing softly at himself for letting his feelings show.

"Yeah, right," Sam said, chuckling, hoisting himself to his feet. "I guess I'd better get out of your way, Mr. Sheriff. I wouldn't want to hinder the fine workings of the law here."

But Rafe wasn't paying any attention. He frowned, looking toward the door into the rest room. "What the hell is taking so long?" he complained. Then his gaze fell on his own desk. "And what happened to her purse?"

Sam stared at the empty spot, as well. "I don't know. It was there when . . ."

Rafe was already striding toward the bathroom. "Cami!" he called, banging on the door with his fist. "Cami?"

He jerked the door open and stared into the empty room. "She's gone," he said softly, then thundered, "She's gone! Where the hell . . . ?"

They yelled for a few minutes, at each other and at themselves, tearing through the office and on outside, surprising a crowd of children who had been on their way to see the lady behind bars. When the two men came bursting out, the kids scattered, screaming for their lives. Rafe and Sam looked in the distance and in the general store and everywhere else they could think of, but they couldn't find a hint of her.

"Maybe she got a ride up to her car," Rafe suggested, tugging at his hair distractedly.

"Hey, wait a minute," Sam said, slapping his leg. "Didn't I hear the bus go through a little while ago?"

Rafe looked at him skeptically. "The bus? How'd it get through?"

"They've got the highway cleared already."

"They can't have it plowed all the way to Varnstown."

"Sure. They've got those new plows over in Esperanza."

Rafe shook his head, still unbelieving. "I'll go up and check out the car. You go after the bus."

"Okay." Sam headed for his car as Rafe went toward his. "Keep in touch."

"Will do." Rafe turned, his dark eyes haunted. "And listen, Sam? Whatever you do, make sure she doesn't get hurt."

"You got my word on that one, boss." Sam jammed his hat on his head and swung down into the driver's seat. "If I let that little lady get hurt, I'll be out of a job, and probably lying stiff and cold in my own hogan by nightfall," he muttered to himself. "And then my parents would have to look for a new place to live." He shook his head resolutely. "No, sir. I won't let anything happen to her."

Cami was fidgeting in her seat. It hadn't taken her long to have second thoughts about this wild flight she was on. How hard would it be for Rafe to extradite her from Colorado? Would she be a fugitive the rest of her life, always looking over her shoulder to see if she were being followed? And what about her car? She'd left it behind.

She'd never dreamed she would be able to get this far away without them catching her. And to tell the truth, she was somewhat dismayed. Rafe was a very annoying man and she was still darn mad at him, but he was...he was...

"He's the best man you've met in years and you know it," she told herself sternly.

When she thought about the collection of bozos she'd dated most of her life, she had to cringe. For instance, there was Stanley. Good old Stanley. She'd gone with him for years, from college right on into her mid-twenties. And every so often, Stanley would reaffirm his plan to marry her and start a family, and then, like clockwork, he would put it off again. Looking back, she could hardly believe she'd been so gullible for so long. It took her four long years to figure out he was never going to do what he'd promised. When was it that she'd begun to fall out of love with the man? She couldn't tell. All she knew was, one day she'd woken and stared at her ceiling and known she had to cut him loose. Their relationship was going nowhere.

She'd spent the next year or so making up for lost time, dating every man she met, until she'd realized this frenzied activity was getting her nowhere. And that was when she'd retreated to her fern journal, giving the passion to her work that she longed to give to a man and a house full of kids.

Rafe was the first man she'd met in years who she could possibly picture as the father of her children. Too bad she'd fallen for someone so out of reach.

Sunk in her own thoughts, she didn't notice the beautiful scenery of the snow-covered landscape that was racing past her window. It took the sticky hand of a little boy to bring her back to her senses.

"Hey, lady. Hey, lady," said the little boy, his huge blue eyes gazing at her solemnly. "Are you going to cry?"

Startled, she looked at him and laughed. He was about three or four, with a mop of red hair and a turned-up nose that was just beginning to be covered with freckles. "No, I'm not going to cry," she assured him. "I was just thinking very hard."

He nodded as though he knew exactly what she meant. Leaning in on the empty seat beside her with his elbows, he confided in her. "I was just thinkin', too. I was thinkin' 'bout tigers."

"Tigers." She nodded. Why not? "There aren't too many tigers around here."

"Nope." His chin rested in his sticky fists. "Tigers live in the jungle."

"So I've heard."

"I'm going to the jungle."

"Are you?"

"Yup. My dad's gonna take me."

"Lucky you," she said, smiling at him. "And what are you going to do in the jungle?"

He thought for a moment, frowning, then an idea lit his face with happiness. "I'm going to make a tiger be my pal."

"Good luck," she said, but at the same time, a voice from toward the middle of the bus called, "Timmy? Timmy, where are you?"

"Is that your mother?" she asked the boy.

He pretended he had heard neither the call from the forward seats, nor Cami's question. "I'm going to wear big boots in the jungle," he mused, but his attention was wandering, and he turned and looked at another woman sitting alone across the aisle.

"Tigers live in the jungle," he told her, abandoning Cami.

Cami smiled. Yes, this was where she'd come in.

But Timmy didn't have time to cultivate her neighbor. His mother's voice called again, and this time it had a certain edge he obviously recognized as one he didn't want to cross. Turning from the woman across the aisle, he bounded away.

Cami looked over and smiled at the woman. "Cute little guy," she noted.

"Yeah, he is."

The woman didn't smile back, but she didn't seem unfriendly. Cami gazed at her for a moment, taking stock. She really seemed to be overdoing it for the day after a snowstorm. The tightly wound scarf and dark glasses were reminiscent of movie stars from the fifties trying to go incognito. All Cami could really make out was the hard little mouth and small, square hands, twitching nervously. Nevertheless, she was warmed by the presence of her fellow traveler. She sensed a potential ally here—someone to drink a cup of tea with at the next rest stop.

"Do you have any kids?" the woman asked, leaning across the empty seat beside her to get closer to Cami.

"No." She shook her head.

"I've got a couple. But I don't see them much. Don't have too much time for kids in my line of work."

Cami nodded but was saddened by her answer. After all these years wishing she could be a mother herself, she couldn't imagine leaving her kids behind for any mere job. "What is it that you do?"

"Travel. A lot."

If she wasn't going to be any more explicit than that, Cami certainly wasn't going to push her.

"Heading for Denver?" she asked instead.

"Nope. I'm going farther than that." She was chewing gum, her mouth working like a piston. "How about you?"

"I'm getting off in Denver. I'm on my way to a baby shower."

"Baby shower." She gave a cough of laughter. "Do people still have those?"

"Some do." She felt a pang. She remembered suddenly that she'd left the wrapped present for the new baby in her car, stuck in a snowbank. How could she arrive at the shower without a present? For just a moment, it seemed impossible, overwhelming. Then the bus skidded and every passenger let out a small shriek as it regained its footing and went on.

"What do you think?" the woman across the aisle said behind her hand. "Are we going to make it there alive, or is this guy going to hang us out over a canyon somewhere?"

"Well, I'm sure he doesn't want to crash any more than we do."

"No, they never do. That's for sure."

The woman was strange but friendly. Cami looked over, noted the wisps of blond hair escaping from her tightly wound scarf, and wondered what she really looked like.

"My name's Cami," she said, sticking out her hand. "I'm from Los Angeles."

"Oh yeah? I'm…uh…" There was a distinct pause. The panes of her sunglasses were dark, but Cami could have sworn she saw her eyes shift. "Lucky," she said quickly. "Lucky Cruise. I'm from…uh…a little town in Arizona. You've never heard of it."

"Near Phoenix?"

"No. No, this little town is down in the south end of the state." She moved restlessly. "Actually, I hardly know the place myself. I was born there, but I've never lived more than six months in one place in my life. So I guess you could say, I'm from all over."

"Oh."

Cami's gaze fell on the magazine in Lucky's lap. It was open to an ad for a contest. "Lucky Sweepstakes!" it proclaimed. "Win a cruise."

Lucky…cruise….

That was funny. Those were the same words….

Oh. She'd made up the name. Now why in the world would she do a thing like that? Whoever she was, Cami wasn't going to tell anyone. Not while she was riding along on a bus in the middle of nowhere.

People were strange. She supposed she ought to be more careful about talking to strangers. One never knew. Most people were just fine, of course, but all you would need would be one nut case. One Billie Joe Calloway…

She felt as though she'd just been struck by lightning. It couldn't be. The coincidence was just too unlikely. And yet…

Her heart was thumping. Adrenaline was pumping through her veins. There was no doubt the woman was trying to hide her identity. Why would she do that? Who was

Cami to her, after all? Why would she bother? Un-less . . . unless she had serious reasons. Unless she was run-ning away from serious charges.

What if this was Billie Joe Calloway?

No. It couldn't be. Her imagination was running away with her. After all, what was the evidence? The fact that she was hiding her identity? Probably a dozen women were do-ing the same thing in this state at that very moment.

She was overreacting. This was ridiculous. What would a woman like Billie Joe be doing on a bus, anyway?

What should she do? Tell the driver of her suspicions? What if he didn't handle it tactfully? She didn't want Lucky to shoot up the bus the way Billie Joe had shot up that place in Laughlin. And anyway, she was probably wrong. This person wasn't Billie Joe Calloway at all. Just think how embarrassing it could be to accuse someone of something like that and then be proved wrong.

"Yeah," she said to herself softly. "Just like a sheriff we all know and love."

Oh, boy. This was really weird. What if this really was her? What could she do to test her theory? Call out "Hey, Billie Joe" and see if she turned her head? And what if she also turned a gun this way? That wouldn't work.

There was a small, buzzing sound and the woman calling herself Lucky pulled a cellular phone from her purse. Cami felt a pang of remorse that she didn't have her own phone with her. But she turned away. She wasn't going to listen in on Lucky's conversation. That would be rude.

Still she couldn't help but overhear some of it.

"...told you not to call me...I don't know...tell him to get the hell out of...tell him not to...you tell him Billie Joe said so, that's who...."

She gasped inside, but no sound made it out. Staring blindly out the window, she forced herself to remain calm, despite the fact that her heart was beating off the chart. It was Billie Joe! It really was! Now what was she going to do?

"Comin' into Bodine," the driver called out from the front of the bus. "You all will have exactly ten minutes to stretch your legs and grab a snack at the little coffee shop. Then we'll be on our way, no waiting for anyone."

Okay, she had her plan. The moment the bus stopped, she'd jump off and find a public telephone. She'd call Rafe, let him know where his criminal was—the real criminal— and then...well, she didn't know what then. That was as far as the plan went for now. If she could get through that, she would go on to the next step.

Things went like clockwork. The phone booth was just steps from where the bus stopped. She dialed information for Rafe's office number, wrote it down quickly, though her hand was shaking badly, and punched in the numbers. It rang twice, and then Rafe's voice came on, asking that she leave her name and number and the exact nature of her business with the sheriff.

Cami stood where she was, stunned. Call the sheriff's station and you get an answering machine? She'd never heard of such a thing. Quickly she gave her message. "I can't believe this! An answering machine? Where are you, Rafe? I think I've found the real Billie Joe, and I need you. I'm on the bus to Denver. Hurry!"

She hung up and stared at the phone. Outrage chased panic through her system. What now? She looked nervously toward the little coffee shop with its fogged-up windows and decided she might find someone inside she could tell about this, someone who would give her some idea of what she could do.

But the moment she stepped inside the muggy room, Lucky hailed her.

"Hey, honey, come on over here. I got you a cup of coffee."

"Oh." She looked around the room, but there was no sign of anything to save her from this. Other passengers filled the booths and tables, but no one looked up, no one looked friendly. No one except the woman she was sure was Billie Joe. "Okay," she said, trying to smile. "Thanks."

Slipping down onto the chair beside the woman, she cupped the mug of coffee in her hands. If nothing else, it was warm.

"Did you see that guy with the goatee, the one who's been sitting up by the driver?" Lucky leaned close, telling secrets. "He put his hand on my shoulder when I was getting off. Can you believe that?" Her tiny mouth twisted with disdain. "The nerve of the guy. You can't tell about people, especially when you're traveling." Her hand slid into her purse and she pulled something out. "That's why I always carry this little baby whenever I take a trip," she said, and suddenly Cami could see that it was a small, pearl-handled revolver, and her mouth went dry.

"Go on," Lucky urged, pressing the gun into Cami's hand. "Hold her. Get the feel of her. You ought to have something like this, too, honey. You just never know."

"You just never know," Cami echoed mindlessly, staring at the dark, heavy object in the palm of her hand. A gun. She was holding a gun.

Something moved in the edge of her line of vision, and she looked up. A tall man in a uniform stood in the doorway, staring straight at her from behind reflective sunglasses.

Sam! she thought, staring but not saying anything out loud.

His face didn't change, didn't show any sign of recognition. Abruptly he turned and left the café, disappearing around the corner.

Cami sat where she was, staring after him. Sam had been standing in that doorway. He'd seen her sitting here with a gun in her hand, and he'd turned around and walked away.

Lucky snatched the gun back and Cami realized she was just as shocked. "I don't get it," she muttered, jamming the weapon back into her purse. "He must have seen the gun in your hand. Why didn't he do something? What kind of cop would just walk away from something like that?''

Why indeed? Why didn't he greet her? Why didn't he come over and say something? Why did he turn on his heel like that? She couldn't think of one good answer to any of those questions.

''Maybe he's used to seeing women with guns,'' she murmured, feeling very alone.

''Are you kidding?'' Lucky said with a shiver. ''They use any excuse they can find to get you. They just love locking people away.'' She leaned close and said confidentially, ''You ever been in jail, Cami?''

Cami blinked. ''Actually, I have,'' she said with a sense of wonder.

''Really? You don't look the type. But, like they say, you never can tell.''

''I may not be the type,'' Cami said, realizing she now fulfilled a whole new category in life, ''but I was there.''

''You can tell me all about it later,'' Lucky said, rising and pulling on Cami's sleeve to get her to rise, as well. ''Right now, we've got to get out of here.''

''We do?'' She felt bewildered but followed her new friend willingly enough.

''Sure,'' Lucky said, leading her out the door of the café. ''He may be coming back with reinforcements. He could drag your buns in, honey. Carrying a concealed weapon.''

''But it wasn't concealed,'' Cami said shakily. ''It was out in the open.''

''Oh, trust me. They'll lock you up and throw away the key.'' She looked up and down the street cagily. ''If we stick to the alleyways—''

''Look.'' Cami pointed to the police car that was heading out of town. ''He's leaving.'' A feeling of cold desolation swept over her as the red taillights turned the corner. Sam was leaving. Why? Because he'd seen her with a gun in her hand? Did he think she was really Billie Joe? What?

"I can't believe it," Lucky said, shaking her head in wonder. "But that's good for us. We can go ahead and take the bus."

Cami hardly heard her. Her mind was in turmoil, but she knew one thing. She had to stay with this woman, keep an eye on her. If she was ever going to prove her own innocence, it was going to be with Lucky—or Billie Joe—as Exhibit A.

"Now listen," Lucky said as they boarded the bus. "You and me gotta stick together."

They slipped back into their seats, but Lucky settled a few things into her tote bag and made her way across the aisle, slumping beside Cami in the vacant seat.

"Okay, here's the plan," she said, leaning close. "The next town we stop in, we get off, we hit the local gas station, and we're gone."

Cami blinked at her, slightly stunned. "What do you mean, hit a gas station?" she whispered.

"Rob it, of course." She licked her lips as though relishing the prospect of a little action. "Liberate some money from the till. See, I had to leave my car behind. It was brand-new, too, the sweetest green Mustang. I'll never see that baby again." She shook her head sadly. "But we'll do okay. Like I say, we'll get some dough at the nearest gas station, then, see, we can grab a car, because they're bound to have some in for repairs."

Cami was shaking her head, amazed at the cool confidence of the woman, feeling slightly sick to her stomach. "I don't think I could do that."

Lucky took hold of her arm. "Honey, you gotta do it. We're in this together."

And in a strange way, she was right.

Lucky went on talking in her low, sibilant voice, but Cami didn't pay much attention. Her mind was full of questions, and she felt curiously numb. This was so very odd. Twenty-four hours before, she'd never heard of Billie Joe, and she'd certainly never had any contact with any people from the criminal side of life. *Well,* she thought suddenly. *Except for those people at the underground paper I worked for in my youth.*

Still, she'd never done anything illegal that she knew of. Then she'd been accused of being this modern day Bonnie without her Clyde. And now here she was, one of the gang. The whole thing was insane.

How had she come to this? She looked at Lucky to her left, chattering on behind her dark glasses, her mouth working as hard on the words as it was on her wad of gum. And then she looked to the right, out the window, at the miles and miles of untouched white snow, the endless blue skies, the mountains.

Why had Sam turned and left her? What was he telling Rafe right now? That he'd been right? That she wasn't worth following?

She had to show him that she wasn't Billie Joe, and the only way she could see to do that at the moment was to stick to this Lucky person like glue, stick until she could find a cop to turn her in to. Did that mean she was going to end up involved in knocking over a gas station? Oh, good Lord!

They rolled into the somewhat larger town of Creosote and she looked out at the stores lining the street, cringing when she noted a gas station on a corner. Lucky tapped her shoulder and nodded toward it, smiling.

"It's about ten minutes to the Colorado state line from here," she whispered. "We've got it made, believe me."

Oh yes, they certainly did. Cami groaned silently, but prepared to disembark with her new pal. As they reached the front of the bus, she stopped and turned.

"You know what? I haven't paid the driver for my ticket yet. If we're leaving the bus here, I've got to do that."

"What?" The gum hung in midair as Lucky stared at her. "Are you nuts?" she hissed. "Get while the gettin's good, honey."

"No." There were some things Cami would not do, even on the dawning of her entry into a life of crime. "It wouldn't be right not to pay him." She fumbled in her purse while Lucky fumed by her side. Once her transaction was completed and they were off the bus, Lucky began to voice her doubts.

"I don't know if you're cut out for this, honey," she said from the side of her mouth. "Maybe you'd better let me handle this on my own."

If only she could agree. "No," she said quickly. "Oh no. I want to stay with you. I . . . I promise I'll hold up my end of the project. Really."

Lucky gazed at her doubtfully, but finally she shrugged. "Okay. Let's get going. That station was over this way."

They started down the street, Cami's heart thumping painfully in her chest. This was crazy and she knew it, but what else could she do? Until she found a way to contact the police, she was stuck with Lucky.

Small storefronts lined either side of the street, a five-and-dime, a boutique, a fresh-produce shop. There weren't many people out, despite the nice weather. The street had been plowed, and most of the sidewalk cleared, but there were still patches of snow, and Cami slipped in places. And then—the sign for the gas station loomed ahead. She could see the attendant taking money from a customer. He was an old man and he limped when he walked. Was Lucky going to hurt him?

Her stomach felt like a rock. This was really going to happen. She was going to be involved in a robbery, and things were going to explode, things she would have no control over. Her movements became stiff and automatic, and her breathing seemed labored. Was she going to be able to do it? Was she?

Lucky grabbed her arm, her mouth working on the gum at a furious pace. "Okay, honey. I'll start up a conversation with the old man. You sort of slink back into the of-fice and . . ."

A tremor ran through her and she knew the truth. No. She couldn't do it. She couldn't risk something happening to the old man, she couldn't risk someone getting hurt. It wasn't right, and she couldn't justify it, not even in order to clear her own name.

She stopped short just before the corner across from the station, stopped short and turned to tell Lucky to stop, as well, but the words never made their way out of her mouth. Something happened before she could begin.

Suddenly something was dragging her back, and as her mind tried to encompass what was happening, she realized she'd been grabbed from behind. Turning, squirming, she saw Sam's familiar face, and she relaxed, flooded with re-lief. Sam had her. It was going to be okay.

But her relief didn't last long. As she turned back toward the street, she could see Rafe confronting Lucky, and as though in slow motion, she saw the metal of the gun flash in Lucky's hand.

"No!" she screamed, trying to twist her way out of Sam's grip. Rafe was in danger, and that was all she could see. She had to get to him.

A gunshot rang out and she froze, paralyzed with fear, but Rafe had reached Lucky and was wrestling the gun from her hand. She hadn't hit him. He was all right. Cami slumped against Sam, weak with a new and deeper sense of relief.

Suddenly there seemed to be policemen everywhere. Lucky—or Billie Joe, if that was really who she was—was being arrested and Rafe was striding toward Cami, his face hard, his mouth a slash of anger across his dark jaw.

"Come here," he ordered, taking her from Sam. He took her by the arm and pulled her roughly. She stumbled along at his side, in a daze and not sure what he was doing. But willing to go along with him. Utterly willing.

They turned a corner and were behind the building when he swung her around and took her in his arms, holding her close. Then he drew back and looked down at her, his hands framing her face.

"Are you okay?" he asked, his voice low and husky, his gaze searching her face. "You didn't get hurt?"

She shook her head. Her throat was tight. She knew words wouldn't come out right now. But her eyes filled with tears, and his image swam before her.

He swore softly and then his mouth was on hers. She clung to him, lost to anything else. He crushed her to him, imprisoned in his embrace, and his mouth plundered her, took from her as though he were starving and she held all the sustenance he needed. She gave him everything she had, offered herself up, didn't even try to hide her feelings. She was still shaken by how close he'd come to being shot. In that terrifying moment, she'd realized how much the world would lose without him. It was something she didn't want to have to face.

Finally he forced himself back. Slowly he let her go, as though it were a very difficult thing to do. But he still held her face between his hands, examining her eyes, her swollen lips, her crystal-clear skin, as though to find an answer to a question that had been puzzling him for a long, long time.

"Why did you leave like that?" he asked her at last. "What made you run?"

Weak with passion and filled with an overwhelming warmth she hardly knew how to identify, she had to make an effort to get words out. "I...it was because you still didn't believe I was Cami Bishop."

He frowned, shaking his head, his fingers lacing into her hair. "Sure I did. I've believed it for a long time."

She bit her lip. Here in the comfort of his protective arms, it was hard to remember just how it had been. But then it began to come back to her, and she glared at him accusingly. "I heard you planning to take me down to Santa Fe for an identity check," she said.

His face changed. "Oh." And then he didn't say anything else, but his expression was pained. "Oh, jeez," he muttered.

Sam had found them and approached during that last exchange, glancing from one to the other and looking apologetic for disturbing them. "Boss, they want you to sign a few papers before we go."

Rafe nodded, releasing Cami and turning away. "All right. See that she gets in my car, okay?"

"Will do." Sam grinned at Cami as Rafe left them. "Shall we go?"

Cami steadied herself, regaining equilibrium with effort. Rafe was a dominating personality to begin with, but when he swept her up in his emotions the way he had just done, it left her shaken and unable to fall gently back to earth without some adjusting. But she did what she could and managed a watery smile for Sam. "Sure." She blinked at the tall deputy. "But first tell me why you left me there in that coffee shop in Bodine."

He threw back his head and laughed. "Rafe told me first priority was that you not get hurt. I saw you with that hard-looking woman, and I sort of thought we might be on to something, but then I saw you holding a gun in your hand, and I decided the best thing to do was get Rafe in on the action before anything went down."

"But she might have gotten away."

He shrugged. "Like I said, Rafe's first priority was you."

She shook her head, not sure she believed that.

He hesitated, as though he might say more, then gestured to her. "Let's go."

Cami nodded, suddenly exhausted. "I feel like I could sleep for about ten days straight."

He led her down the main drag past the cars with lights flashing, past the onlookers, to Rafe's yellow Jeep. Here and there a curious face turned her way, but for the most part, no one noticed. And once they got to the Jeep, they had left the crowd behind.

"What happened to the police unit?" she asked as she opened the door and got into the passenger's seat.

"Don't you think a bunch of blue-and-whites passing the bus might have tipped Billie Joe off?" he said.

She nodded, convinced by his impeccable logic. "So you realized she was with me."

"Rafe got your message on the answering machine."

"And he finally had to admit he had arrested the wrong woman," she said, a tiny spark of bitterness in her tone.

"Hey, listen, Cami," Sam said, turning back to look at her earnestly. "Don't you get it? Don't you understand why Rafe was planning to take you down to Santa Fe?"

She blinked at him, not sure she had a clue. "To check out my identity." What else could it be?

He made a face. "Don't be an idiot. He knew damn well who you were by then. Don't you see? He knew he was going to have to let you go, that you would be out of here like a shot once you were released."

Reaching out, he touched her cheek and grinned. "He wanted to buy more time alone with you, lady. Can't you see that?"

See it? She could barely comprehend it.

He laughed and turned on his heel, going back to the group of police in the center of the street, and she sat where she was, stunned once again. Was it true? She didn't dare think about it too hard. If it was true...if it was...

Eight

Cami woke with a start. The doorbell was ringing. Rubbing her eyes, she had to work to get a fix on where she was. But then she remembered. Rafe's bed. A languorous sense of sensuality came over her and she snuggled down into the thick covers. Rafe's bed. If only he were in it.

He'd been silent on the drive back from Creosote, and instead of going back to the sheriff's station, he'd pulled up in front of his own house. Still uncommunicative, he'd led her in and brought out fresh towels for her, gesturing toward the shower.

"Go ahead and take a bath," he told her stiffly. "The bedroom is through that door. Get some sleep. I'll handle the paperwork to get you untangled from all this."

Untangled. Strange word. She wanted to be set free of the criminal charges, but she wasn't so sure she wanted to cut everything loose. She stood in the middle of the floor, feeling tired, feeling just a little lost. "Does that mean I'm not arrested any longer?"

A dark look came over his face, and for a moment she was afraid he was angry with her. He started to say something, then seemed to swallow his words.

"That's right," he said at last, not meeting her gaze. "You're free to go any time you want. But you're going to need your car." Turning, he started toward the front door. "In the meantime, get some sleep. I'm sure you're exhausted. You've had a rough twenty-four hours."

Twenty-four hours. How could so much have happened in such a short time? She watched him walk away and she wanted to call him back. But what was there to say?

So when he'd left her, she'd taken a long, hot bath and found one of his shirts to wear before falling into his bed and sleeping like a log for about four hours.

The bell rang again and she sighed. She supposed she was going to have to answer it, even though she didn't have a robe and was wearing nothing but an old dress shirt of Rafe's. Sliding out of the high bed, she looked around for something to cover herself with. Rafe's robe was hanging on the back of the door. That would do, despite the fact it had a football logo over the pocket. She tugged it on and padded to the front door.

"Hi." A bright-eyed young woman greeted her, her black hair in a long braid down her back. In her hands she held a covered casserole dish.

"Hi," Cami said back. "If you're looking for Rafe...uh, the sheriff..."

The young woman shook her head, smiling. "I'm Sally," she said. "I came over to see you."

"Me?"

She nodded, her eyes dancing. "I had to come over to find out what the heck is going on." She cocked her head to the side. "The children told me the sheriff had a lady in a cage. And Junior said he informed them he was planning to keep her there all spring." She laughed. "I guess that was you. And if you're staying all spring, I thought we ought to get to know each other.''

''Oh.'' Cami smiled as well. This was the Sally she'd heard the men mention. ''I'm not in the cage any longer, as you can see, and I'm definitely not staying all spring. But you might as well come on in and we can get acquainted.''

She watched, slightly edgy, as Sally swept in and made straight for the kitchen with her covered dish. She was remembering now how Sally had sent messages inviting Rafe over to her house. She'd definitely had the impression Sally was after Rafe. So what was she doing here and what exactly was the purpose of this visit?

''How did you know I was here?'' she asked, following her into the kitchen and watching as she opened the refrigerator and looked for space.

''I weaseled it out of Sam,'' Sally said cheerfully, shoving the dish into an empty space. ''Lasagna,'' she noted. ''Fully cooked. Just needs to be warmed about half an hour before you're ready to eat.'' She closed the refrigerator door with a snap.

Should she thank her? Cami hesitated, not sure if the meal was supposed to be for her or for Rafe—or for both of them.

''Now,'' Sally said firmly, dropping into a kitchen chair. ''What's the deal here?''

''Excuse me?'' Cami raised an eyebrow and looked at the woman questioningly.

Sally smiled at her. ''Don't be offended, please. I didn't mean anything by being so abrupt. But we don't have much time. And you see, I really care about Rafe.'' She shook her head and shrugged. ''We all do around here. So we want to know what your intentions are.''

''My intentions?'' Flabbergasted, Cami sank into a chair across the table from her. ''What on earth are you talking about?''

Sally pursed her lips. "Well, let me give you a little background. We had an opening for a sheriff about three years ago, and we were having trouble filling it. Not many men with the qualifications we were requiring wanted to be stranded out here so far away from city excitement. And then, Rafe arrived."

"He told me he'd worked in Los Angeles."

"Yes. And he was looking for a change. But it was more than that." Getting up, she scanned the room, then looked out into the living room. "I don't suppose he had a picture of a woman in his bedroom, did he?" she asked.

Cami shook her head. "No. I would have noticed if he did."

She nodded, sitting back down. "He's got a picture of her somewhere. Sam's seen it."

"Oh, I think I have, too," Cami said. "At least, there was a picture of a woman I found him holding in the office."

"That's her. Sam found out a few facts from buddies who worked in L.A. She was his partner. They were madly in love."

For some reason, Cami was shaking. Something deep inside didn't want to hear about this. But she had to know. "What happened to her?" she asked softly.

"She was killed in the line of duty. They were together at the time."

Cami closed her eyes. "Oh, my God."

"Yes, it was horrible. And he was...well, I guess you could have called him something of a broken man when he first came here. He never talked about it to anyone, but we knew something was wrong, and then, as I say, Sam found out a few things."

Cami wanted to go to him. Everything inside her ached to comfort him. And yet, this was something he didn't want to share with anyone. She knew instinctively that any expressions of sympathy would be repulsed, and with anger. She would have to leave it alone. If she could.

"The first year, he did a great job, but he was so closed to us, it was hard to get to know him. Things got better over the months, and now, he's a real part of this community. But there's a lingering melancholy to him. And he keeps very much to himself."

Cami nodded. She'd seen that.

"The children adore him. The only times I've really seen him lose all traces of sadness are when he's with the children."

"Yes, I've seen that, too."

"But in these years..." Sally hesitated, searching Cami's face for her reaction. "In all this time, you're the first woman he's let get this close."

"This close?" If this was the closest he got, things were worse than she'd thought.

"Sure. I mean, into his house. And from what I hear, he kissed you."

Cami rolled her eyes. "How did you know that?"

"This is a very small town." She sighed, then smiled brightly. "I've been hoping it would be me, you know. But it seems to be you. So I ask again, what are your intentions?"

Cami bit her lip. "Sally," she said slowly, "I appreciate how you feel about him. And I'm grateful that you told me about...about his friend being killed. But whatever has happened between the two of us is...well, it's between the two of us."

Sally nodded. "I know that. What I'm trying to do here is to make you aware of what a special person he is. He deserves the best." Reaching out, she took Cami's hand and added in a choked voice, "Don't hurt him. Okay?"

Cami opened her mouth but there didn't seem to be anything she could say that could answer that, and when she noticed the tears brimming in Sally's eyes, she squeezed her hand tightly. "I don't think there is any need to worry about that," she said, feeling a little teary herself. "He hasn't made any real sign that he . . . well, that he wants anything special from me. You know what I mean? He kissed me, yes, but it was just one of those things."

"Just one of those crazy things," Sally echoed, studying her eyes. Finally she seemed to see what she'd been looking for, and her mouth turned up at the corners. Drawing back her hand, she rose. "Okay, I've said my piece. I'll get out of your hair." She smiled over her shoulder as she made her way to the front door. "Good luck," she said.

Cami hugged it to herself. She was going to need it.

Rafe paused at his own front door, hesitating. He knew Cami was inside, and everything in him wanted to go to her. But he had to prepare himself. This wasn't going to be easy.

He'd moved up here to the mountains because he'd wanted to live an uncomplicated life, and for three years, everything had worked out fine. Then Cami had wandered into his sights and all hell had broken loose.

It was crazy, the way he felt about her. It filled his mind, set off his emotions in a way he couldn't explain. It couldn't be love. Could it?

That question tortured him, because it couldn't be. He'd given all his love to Janie, and that couldn't be changed. But it was something close. He liked her a lot. And he wanted her. Oh, God, yes, he wanted her.

So he had to be careful. He had to watch every step. She must never know how he felt. And he couldn't allow himself to act on it. After three years of perfect control, he was about to lose it all if he didn't watch it. Steeling himself, he made his way inside his own house.

He couldn't tell where she was at first. Setting down his briefcase, he glanced into his own empty bedroom, then followed the sound of humming to the kitchen. And there she stood at the counter, throwing together a salad in a large wooden bowl.

He drew in a ragged breath. This wasn't going to be easy. She looked good enough to give up food for, with the afternoon sun shining in her golden hair and the fabric of the shirt outlining the sway of her breasts. Something choked in his throat, and he was afraid it was his own sense of pure animal lust. He was going to have to fight that. It wouldn't be fair to... to...

To throw her down on the kitchen table and make wild, passionate love to her. He might as well face it. That was exactly what he wanted to do. *Wanted—hell!* Needed. Craved. Required in order to keep from going mad. He clenched his fists at his sides and fought it hard.

Looking up, she saw the expression on his face and mistook it for surprise that she was still there. She smiled at him.

"What did you think I was going to do, run away again?" she asked.

But he didn't return her smile. He was too busy keeping himself under control to let out even that much weakness. Just one strand gone, and it would all go to hell in a hand basket. "I've got your car out front," he told her stiffly. "Sam and I checked it out. It runs fine." He hesitated, then forced himself to add, "You're free to go anytime."

She turned away and went back to tearing apart lettuce. "Free as a bird," she murmured.

He studied how she looked in his dress shirt, with her long legs bare, her toes cute and pink, and he took a deep breath. He had to get this woman covered up. "Listen, your suitcase is in the trunk of the car. You want me to bring it in?"

She smiled serenely. "Yes, thank you. Then I can change. That would be nice."

"That would be a shame," he muttered to himself in disagreement as he turned away. Much as he liked the look of her this way, she would be better off in something else. He needed her more fully dressed or this whole charade wasn't going to work at all.

He came back in with the suitcase and set it down at the edge of the kitchen.

"I fixed dinner," she told him happily, putting the salad in the middle of the table. He noticed she'd set it. Two place settings, with yellow mats and green napkins and his stainless steel flatware.

"You didn't have to do that."

"I know." She made a face. "Well, okay, I didn't really fix it all. In fact, your friend Sally came by with a lasagna. So I guess I'll have to give most of the credit to her."

"Oh." He glanced at the oven and then looked at Cami, curious how the two women had taken to each other. "That was nice of her."

"Yes."

They stared at each other. He wanted to suggest she go ahead and change, and hurry up about it, too, but the words wouldn't come. He didn't look at her legs, but he couldn't help but be aware of them. He'd never been much of a leg man before, but these legs were something special. She was going to have to put them where he couldn't see them, one way or another.

He was staring too hard and she wasn't sure why, but it was making her very uncomfortable. She could sense he had something to say but didn't want to say it. Still, someone had to say something or they would go on standing here forever. The longer the silence lasted, the harder it was going to be to break. She turned and pretended to check the salad.

"So," she said, attempting to sound casual. "What has happened? Is Lucky Cruise really Billie Joe?"

He blinked, as though startled by the sound of her voice, but in seconds, he was back to normal. "Uh...yes," he answered, giving his head a quick shake and turning to look away. "Yes, she is, tattoo and all."

Cami swung around to face him, her eyes wide. "You saw her tattoo?"

He shook his head. "Not me. I left that to the proper authorities in Santa Fe."

Now, why did that give her a sense of relief? She had no idea. Billie Joe's tattoos had nothing at all to do with her. "Oh. So you weren't in on the great unveiling."

"No."

"What do you think is going to happen to her?"

"She'll be charged and tried." He took a step closer. "Don't worry about her. She'll land on her feet. People like that always do."

But that wasn't what was on his mind. Whatever was bothering him was still there. She stood very still, waiting. He had something he wanted to say to her, and she wasn't sure she wanted to hear it. If it was so difficult for him to get out, was it also going to be difficult for her to hear?

"Cami." He wanted to touch her, to hold her when he said it, but he didn't dare. If he took her in his arms, there was no guarantee he would ever be able to let her go again. But he had to say something. It wasn't fair to her not to. He had nightmare images floating through his mind, images he couldn't shake. He'd put a woman he cared for in the line of fire—again. This was a syndrome he didn't seem to be able to avoid. The best thing for her would be to go, get away from him, and do it fast. He swallowed hard. "Cami, I have to tell you something."

She nodded, silently waiting, her eyes wide and apprehensive.

He hesitated, not sure how to put it into words, then said quietly, "I'm sorry."

She blinked. Perhaps she hadn't heard him properly. "What?"

He took a deep breath and repeated it. "I said I'm sorry."

That was it? She gazed at him, bewildered. "What are you sorry about?"

For caring for you. For mistrusting you. For putting you in harm's way. For wishing I could hold you in my arms right now. For everything. "For what you've been through since last night," was what he finally told her aloud. He shrugged, his eyes haunted. "It was all my fault."

She shook her head, still not sure she was clear on the issue. "You were just doing your job."

"True. But that's no excuse. It was still my fault."

Fingers playing with the collar of the shirt she was wearing, she studied him silently. The man was an enigma to her. She wasn't sure what it all meant, why he'd brought her to his home like this, put her into his bed. On the one hand, she thought they'd reached a certain level in the feelings they'd expressed between them and that his actions were evidence that they really shared something. But now she wasn't so sure. Maybe he just felt guilty. Maybe he just wanted forgiveness. Or maybe he just wanted to make her comfortable so she wouldn't sue him for false arrest.

No, that wasn't it and she knew it. Still, it was annoying. Why did they have to play this game of cat and mouse all the time? Why couldn't he admit he was attracted to her, even to himself?

She knew the answer to that, as well. It was because of the woman in the picture, the one who'd died. How was she going to yank him out of the past and make him live in the present?

The answer was, maybe she wasn't. Maybe that was what he was trying to tell her with his strange apology and his cool demeanor. Maybe he just wanted her to go.

"You're forgiven," she said abruptly, turning and walking into the living room. "And thanks for getting my car down off the mountain." She turned to see if he'd followed her out of the kitchen, somewhat surprised to see that he hadn't used it as an opportunity to escape to another part of the house. But he still looked strange. "I suppose I should pick up my journey right where I left off," she suggested, hoping he would tell her he wouldn't hear of it.

"Now?" was all he said.

She sighed, shoulders sagging. "Well, I should get going. I've got a long drive to get to Denver."

He shifted his weight uneasily. "You can't get there tonight."

Why not, Rafe? Because you won't let me go? Please! "There's no storm coming, is there?" she said aloud.

He shook his head and hunched his shoulders. "Not that I know of."

"Well, then, I suppose I could give it a try." She waited, watched, heart racing. *Please,* she whispered silently. *Please.*

His dark eyes were unreadable, though she stared into them for what seemed like eternity, hoping...hoping.... But when he finally spoke, the hope was over. "If you have to go, I guess you'd better get going," he said shortly, looking away.

Her heart sank, and she turned. There wasn't much point in hanging around if she wasn't wanted.

"But I wish you'd wait until morning."

Was that really his voice that had said that, or only wishful thinking? She spun and stared at him, not really sure.

"Why?" she ventured, breathless, searching his dark face for an answer.

He looked uncomfortable and his mouth twisted. "Because it'll be safer."

"Oh." Was that good or not? She wasn't sure, but her heart was beating very quickly, just in case. "Do you want me to stay here until morning?" she asked, trying to pin it down.

He looked into her eyes, but his own gaze was still guarded. "I could go to the office," he suggested warily. "You could have the bedroom all to yourself."

"Oh!" That was just the limit! Her patience snapped with that. What was wrong with the man, anyway?

"Oh!" she cried again, almost stamping her foot in exasperation. She stared up at him, a storm brewing in her eyes. "Why are you doing this?" she demanded, jabbing a finger in his direction. "Are you or are you not the same man who kissed me this afternoon—the man who took me into his arms and held me close? Was that you?"

He looked startled. "Yeah. That was me," he admitted with some reluctance. "You know that."

She threw up her hands. "I thought it was you. But the way you've been acting, I wasn't too sure." She turned as though to leave, as though she were fed up with him.

He grabbed her wrist, snapping her around to face him. For some reason, he felt he had to explain, even though he knew he was heading into rocky waters. "I know I did some...pretty intimate things, but I was just worried about you."

She gazed up at him, her expression softening until her heart was in her eyes. She loved his face, the way the hard planes met in deep grooves, the way his eyes were hard and impenetrable for so much of the time, only to show sudden flashes of excitingly candid emotions that blew her away.

"No kidding," she said softly. "I was worried about you, too." Stepping closer to him, she braved his reserve and laid the flat of her hand against the side of his face, sighing softly. "You could have been killed," she said, gazing at him lovingly, devouring every bit she could.

He felt like a drowning man, but he was rapidly forgetting to care. Taking her hand in his, he pressed the center of her palm to his lips, kissing her. "And so could you," he murmured, wincing when he remembered how scared he'd been when Sam had called in the report that she was with Billie Joe. "If you'd been shot..."

She swayed against him, her eyes half-closed. "But we weren't, neither one of us. We're both still here. We're both alive. And we both still have a life to live."

He frowned, hesitating, his hand in her hair. "What do you mean by that?" he asked.

A shiver of panic scampered down her spine.

"Nothing," she said quickly, putting a finger to his lips. "Don't talk. It only gets us into trouble." Shaking her head, her mouth curved into a shy smile. "Why don't we kiss instead?" she suggested lightly. And instead of waiting for him to take her up on her offer, she rose on her tiptoes and ringed his neck with her arms, clasping her hands behind his head and arching into him. "Please?"

There was no way to resist such an offer. His hands held her as though she were a precious gift, and she immersed herself in his gaze as it warmed and melted and accepted her into its depths. The last thing she saw before her eyes closed was the spark of desire that was finally unleashed in his expression. And then his mouth was on hers and she welcomed him, excited by the tenderness he was showing her, intrigued by the evidence of fire that lit his eyes. She took him in, unfolding for him, opening and deepening, until she had him all, wrapping around him, melting with him, becoming one in the urgency of their mutual need to cling together.

She was moving in a dream. She felt his touch, his fingertips at the base of her throat, capturing the drumbeat of her pulse, the roughness of his unshaved face against her cheek, the pressure of his hard thigh against her leg, the rasping heat of his tongue against hers, and she reveled in it, drinking it all in, feeling as though it were all so new to her, as though she'd never had a man so close before, never felt this intensity, this aching need, this wave of overwhelming affection and desire.

He felt it, too—the newness. She was so fresh, so alive, so...so clean. He wanted to pick her up in his arms and carry her to some better place, someplace away from memories and regrets. She deserved as much.

But what did he deserve? Did he deserve her? A night with her? A day? A week?

Don't talk, she'd said. *It only gets us into trouble.*

Don't think, either, he might have told her back. Closing his eyes, he took in the scent of her, the sweep of her soft hair as it curled about his shoulder, the rounded pleasure of her breast in his hand, the warmth of her breath on his neck, and he shoved thought to the back of his mind. It was better that way.

He did pick her up, but only to carry her to his bed. She lay back in the thick covers and gazed up at him, her blue eyes dreamy, her hair a shimmering mass of gold about her face. She was still wearing his shirt, but it came away easily, and very quickly. She was as lovely to look at as she had been to touch. Her skin seemed to glow, and her breasts were full and irresistible with their soft, tempting lines and pale pink tips. The nipples darkened as he touched her, tightening and rising in a way that made him groan with satisfaction. He touched them gently, then ran his hands over the curve of her hips and down into the center of her heat.

Crying out with the sensation, she reached for him, wanting him close, needing him closer, and her hands began to work on the buttons of his uniform, fumbling with her eagerness. They were going to make love. Nothing could stop them now. For just a moment, he allowed himself to dwell on that fact, but he couldn't find a way to regret it, much less a reason to stop the inevitable flow of events that was leading them both to exactly the result he'd been guarding against. He couldn't find it within himself to resist. Desire for her was like a wave in the ocean. It was sweeping through him, driving everything in front of it, and it was going to stop for nothing and no one. The rush of feeling only paused while he fumbled impatiently to find protection.

They came together like that, too, like two forces of nature meeting and joining, to crash and become one. Hard muscle hit soft flesh, only to be cradled by it, and urged to come again. And again. And again. She gasped out his name, clutching him to her, holding him with fingers that kneaded into his shoulders, demanding more.

He gave her everything he had, took everything she had to offer in return, and when it was finally coming to an end, he held her to him and buried his face in her hair, shuddering with pleasure, weak with relief.

They lay entangled in each other's arms and legs. When she'd finally caught her breath, Cami risked a look into his dark eyes. He was staring at her, looking shell-shocked. Her mouth turned up at the corners.

"Now, was that so bad?" she whispered.

He stared at her for a moment, then began to laugh. She joined him, and they rocked together, laughing wildly, building a joy between them that was almost as satisfying as the lovemaking had been.

We understand each other, she thought to herself as she settled back and looked at him. She ran her hand over his beautiful body. His arms and legs were hard as rocks, muscular without being flamboyant about it. His stomach was flat, his chest smooth and gorgeous. It took her breath away to touch him, to look at him, and in a moment, she realized her caresses were doing much the same to him.

"Are you brave enough to try again?" he asked her, catching hold of her hand and guiding it to where he wanted it most.

She nodded, eyes huge, heart beating, and as his mouth closed on her nipple, she knew this surge of excitement was something she could get used to, very quickly. Used to, and addicted to. "Oh, Rafe," she said, and sighed as she drew him back inside her and began the hot, rhythmic dance that only he could make her do. "Don't ever let go."

They laughed a lot as they dug into the lasagna, making jokes about how hungry they both seemed to be, and anything else that caught their fancy. Their relationship was on a very different plane than it had been before they'd made love. They could be friends, they both discovered, as well as lovers.

They shared the dishwashing and cleanup chores, then took coffee to the living room and sat on the couch, curled together before the fire Rafe had built, talking sleepily. Cami felt a peace she hadn't known for years, a warm contentment she knew wasn't going to last. But she was bound and determined to enjoy it while she had it.

Rafe was wonderful. She knew that for certain now. She was in love with him, and she would do almost anything if only she thought there was any hope that they might be together. There was the difference in their background, but that could be overcome easily. It was hardly a point to be considered. And there was the fact that he liked it here in the wilderness, while she was a city girl. But that, too, was negligible. She would give up the city in a flash, if it meant having him. The last obstacle was the one she knew she could do nothing to overcome. That was Janie, the woman he had loved, the woman he had lost. There was very little she could do to fight a ghost. She didn't know how to begin to try.

But she wanted to know more about him. Getting up from the couch, she began to explore his living room, asking for a running commentary on all the things she found.

"What's this trophy for?"

"Softball. I was on a team last year. Shortstop."

"Were you the champ?"

He grinned. "More like the chump. But we had a lot of fun."

"How about this picture?"

The painting was of a Navaho girl in a heavy velvet dress and adorned with silver beads.

"Sally painted that and gave it to me. It's her little sister. She came in and answered phones for us last summer."

Cami nodded, smiling at the picture. "She looks a lot like Sally."

She walked on around the room, gazing at his treasures, peeking into side rooms, touching things, cataloging everything as though she were memorizing details to furnish future memories. The shelves out here in the living room were filled with huge specimens of glittering minerals, large crystals of amethyst, a plate of smoky quartz spears, a slab of azurite and malachite. On another shelf was a display of Pueblo pottery. And set to the side, all alone, was a small glass bubble with a scene inside, a cheap paperweight that seemed completely out of place with these other magnificent artifacts.

"What's this?" she asked, picking it up and letting the snowflakes swirl. Looking more closely at the little scene, she was struck with how much it reminded her of the snowy expedition they'd shared the night before. The scene looked the same. There were the snow-covered trees, the fallen log, and two little people sliding down a hill. She looked up and met his gaze, wondering if he was making the same connection. "Pretty," she said simply.

He glanced up and a smile played with his wide mouth when he saw what she was holding. "Yes. Some of the kids gave that to me at Christmas," he said.

She held it a moment longer, staring down into the snowy scene, watching the snowflakes gently settle back down. A man who would put a gift given to him by children on the same shelf with his expensive displays couldn't be all bad. She set it down gently. It deserved respect.

Moving on, she looked out his window at the snow, full of nighttime shadows and mysterious shapes, then turned into the interior. He had books stacked to the ceiling in his den. She browsed through them, and then struck gold. A photo album.

"Mind if I take a look?" she asked him.

He hesitated, knowing there were pictures of Janie inside. He never showed those pictures to anyone else. But this was different. He was going to have to share her sometime.

"Sure," he said, though his voice sounded forced.

There were pictures of Rafe in Los Angeles, pictures of his friends, pictures of parties and cops. And then, there were pictures of him with Janie. Slowly Cami turned and brought the book back to the couch, sinking down beside him. "Tell me about her," she said softly, looking at him as though afraid of how he was going to react.

He steeled himself. This had to be done. "Her name is Janie Griego," he said, and they both noted that he had used the present tense. "We were going to get married."

"Sally told me," she said quietly.

He frowned. "How the hell would Sally know about it?"

"Sam told her. He'd heard from people who'd known you in Los Angeles."

He forced himself to calm down. Much as he hated to think of people talking about him, he knew very well that was what people did.

"Did you love her very much?" Cami asked, unable to look into his eyes to find her answer.

"Yes," he said shortly. "She was a wonderful woman."

There. He'd said it. *That one's for you, Janie,* he told her silently, a warm feeling in his chest. It didn't hurt quite as much as he'd expected. It didn't burn in his soul like it once had.

Maybe it would later, he told himself. When he was alone and had time to think. Right now, he didn't want to think. He wanted to have Cami with him, and he couldn't think about Janie. Reaching out, he closed the book.

"Janie is dead," he said evenly. "She died during a gang bust. She took a bullet that should have hit me. I'll never forgive myself for letting it happen."

Cami cried out, reaching for him. "Oh, but you can't blame yourself—"

He stopped her, holding her hand. "I know. I've heard all the arguments. I've made them myself. But that fact remains. She died at my side. And for a long time, I wished I was dead, too.''

"But not anymore?'' Cami asked him, afraid of the answer.

Slowly, he shook his head. "No,'' he said, almost wonderingly. "No, not anymore.''

Her smile was back, the smile that broke out like sunshine on a cloudy day and could light his life with a glow he'd forgotten existed. "Good,'' she said, sighing with relief. She kissed him quickly, firm and hard on the mouth. "Just to remind you,'' she murmured, rising to put the album away.

He wasn't sure what she was reminding him of, but he liked it anyway. He watched her as she left the room, and he couldn't help smiling, too. If he didn't watch out, he would fall head over heels in love with this woman. He'd never known anyone like her.

And then she was back, still smiling at him. "You know what I want to do?'' she said impulsively. "I want to go out and roll around naked in the snow.''

"No, you don't,'' he said dryly as she bounced back down on the couch beside him.

She gave him a playful slug in the shoulder. "Come on,'' she teased. "Wouldn't it be fun?''

"No,'' he said, though he smiled down at her and touched her cheek with his thumb. "It would be cold.''

She sighed. "You're probably right. But it's fun to think about.''

"Tell you what. Why don't you just roll around naked right here on my bed?'' he suggested.

She made a face. "We've done that already.''

He laughed at her. "Like they say, playgirl, those kicks just keep getting harder to find.''

But she was taken with at least part of the idea. "Let's go back out into the snow, like we did last night,'' she said, tugging at his hand. "It was so beautiful. And I'm...I'm going to be leaving in the morning. It's my last chance."

Was it her imagination or had he winced when she'd said she was leaving? She couldn't tell, and it really didn't matter, did it? She was leaving, whether or not he wanted her to go.

"Do you have to go tomorrow?" he asked her.

She nodded, happy he would ask but unable to see a way it could be different. "I can't miss the shower. Not after I've come through all this to get there."

His hand gathered up her curls and gave a soft tug. Tonight was all they had. But that wasn't something to dwell upon now.

"Let's go," he said.

They got into boots and warm clothes and went out into the midnight air. This time they carried plastic saucers for sliding. The moonlight had turned the landscape silver. Instead of the soft powder of the night before, the snow crunched beneath their feet, and they laughed as they ran for the slope.

They rode down the hill again and again, tumbling into the snow and laughing and saying "Shh!" to each other, afraid too much evidence of the fun they were having would bring out crowds of others to join them. And that was the last thing they wanted. Tonight was for the two of them. Alone.

When they were exhausted from the sliding, he led her into the trees until they came to a small clearing lined with rocks. There he sat her down and quickly built a fire to warm her. They sat beside it and rested, her head on his shoulder.

"You still think you want to roll around naked in the snow?" he asked, smiling down into her happy face.

"No!" she cried, shivering. "That was just a California dream on a New Mexico winter's night."

"I thought you'd see the light."

She settled back against him. "It's so beautiful out here," she mused softly, "it makes me dream."

He pulled her into the curve of his arm. "What do you dream about?" he murmured against her hair.

"You mean, besides rolling naked?" She hesitated. Did she dare tell him the truth? What the heck. What did she have to lose, after all? "I dream of being in love. Of getting married to a wonderful man. Of having fat, happy babies and making a family." There. Baby dreams. That was the truth. Let him deal with it. "What do you dream about?" she asked.

"I don't dream," he said abruptly. "I sleep without dreams."

She pulled back to look into his face. "You know very well I'm talking about daydreams," she said, searching his eyes.

He turned his gaze away. "Like I said, I don't dream. I face reality, I live it, and I get through it. Dreams just bring you disappointment."

Her heart ached for him. "That's no way to live, Rafe," she said softly.

He took a deep breath and turned to meet her eyes. "That's the way I live. And I do all right."

"Oh, Rafe." Stretching up, she kissed him, intending tenderness, intending comfort.

But he caught her up into his arms and the kiss quickly became something else, as though they both needed it to blot out that reality he'd bragged that he could face. It started hot and got hotter, until it seemed to set them both on fire—a wildfire, a blazing inferno that swept away thought and inhibitions. The zipper on her borrowed jacket stuck, and he ripped at it, tearing it open so that he could drop inside and lift her sweater, find her breasts. Her breath came harshly in her throat as her hands worked at the belt on his jeans, then the clasp, and they opened each other up like ripe fruit inside husks, and they plunged in greedily, rolling in the snow, living an image of fire and ice, melting everything they touched with the burning ache of their desire. He pushed down her slacks while she tugged on his tight jeans, and then they'd opened up the pathway and found each other. He came inside her like a conqueror, rising above her as she held him, as though he'd found the road to eternal joy and meant to take it right then and there, and she cried out as he entered, thrusting her hips up to meet him, urging him harder, deeper, meeting him with an urgency that was just as intense as his.

"That wasn't me," she said, panting, when their union was complete and the sensation was beginning to fade into mere ecstasy. "I don't know who that woman was."

But he laughed against her neck, pressing soft kisses along her collarbone, because he knew it had been her, knew she'd had that sort of wanton wildness in her all along. And if he played his cards right, he knew he would be able to coax her out again. After all, there was a long night ahead of them.

They woke late, curled together in his bed. The morning light was already turning to midday sun. Cami lay back and enjoyed the feel of him against her. She'd never felt so fulfilled, so refreshed . . . so happy. If only . . . if only . . .

They rose slowly, yawning a lot, and made their way into the kitchen. He made a pot of coffee while she rummaged through the refrigerator.

"Well, let's see," she said, after a moment or two of looking. "About breakfast. How about some nice cold lasagna?"

"Lasagna?" His tone of voice told her that wasn't his idea of breakfast.

She rose and turned to look at him, leaning on the refrigerator door. "Okay, it looks like you actually have a choice. If you don't want lasagna, you can opt for the steak fajita burrito and a slice of slightly aged lemon meringue pie."

"Is that all I've got in there?" He peeked inside and had to admit the cupboard looked pretty bare.

"That's about it," she told him sadly. Then she made a face, gazing at what was left in the pie pan. "Who would have thought meringue would curl up around the edges like that?" she muttered.

He gave her a ferocious frown. "Are you making a comment on my housekeeping?"

"No." She slammed the door shut. "But I am making a comment on the contents of your refrigerator. How can you live like this?"

He shrugged. "I eat at the office. Mrs. Cummins feeds me."

She shook her head and padded back to the bedroom to raid her suitcase. She had a box of shortbread cookies hidden away there, and it turned out they made a lovely breakfast along with the freshly brewed coffee.

But anything would have tasted delicious this morning. It was a magic morning. And she meant to enjoy it, right up to the last minute. They ate, talking and laughing, and made love once again, and then lay together in the bed and talked some more. They took a shower together and chased each other through the house, and then it was time to go.

But as Cami packed her bag and dressed for her departure, she bit her lip and let her thoughts run wild. This was crazy. What was she doing here? She was in love with this man, and yet she was letting him set up this framework wherein they had only this day and no other. And here she'd bought into it. What was the matter with her? Why didn't she make plans to return? Or to have him come visit her in Los Angeles? That was what normal people did.

So she brought it up to him in a perfectly calm and logical fashion, and saw right away her idea wasn't going to fly.

"No," he said shortly, his eyes hardening again, looking impenetrable, as they had when she'd first known him. "I don't think so. It would be best if we just said goodbye and left it at that.''

''Why?'' She shook her head, bewildered. ''Haven't we been good together?''

She could see that he didn't want to answer that, but she wouldn't let him off the hook, and finally he said, ''Cami, it's been great. Better... better than anything I've done in years. But it can't go on.''

''Tell me why.''

He shook his head. ''It's just not right.''

''Not right?'' That was ridiculous. What could he be talking about? ''What do you mean, not right?''

He hesitated. He'd thought she understood, but maybe not. Still, now that he was going to have to put it into words, it seemed difficult even for him.

''It would just be better if you left and forgot about me. I've got my life set here. I need this place. And you need a different sort of life.''

''But...''

''Cami.'' He took her shoulders in his hands and stared down into her eyes. ''You want marriage and babies and a traditional life. You know you do. You've told me so often enough. And that's a life I'm not set up for. Not physically. Not emotionally. Not psychologically. I can't give you what you need—what you deserve.''

And he wouldn't even give her a chance to prove him wrong? She shook her head stubbornly. ''But just to visit...''

''No,'' he told her bluntly, dropping his hands from her shoulders and turning away. ''It would only make things harder.''

Anger stirred in her, replacing sympathy. What was the matter with this man? Was he so in love with his guilt that he couldn't let it go?

''For whom? For you?''

''For both of us.''

"Oh, I finally get it," she said crisply. "It's not that you love it so much out here in the wilderness. You're here because it's the closest thing you could find to going into the priesthood, isn't it? You're still mourning Janie. You've dedicated your life to mourning her. And nothing's going to make you give that up."

He raised his head and stared right into her blue eyes. Her heart beat wildly. She wasn't at all sure what he was going to do. Finally he turned, as though dismissing her.

"I'll take your bag out to the car," he said. Her words had cut close to the truth, but there was more to it than that. Wasn't there? Or was he letting himself get bogged down in thinking that had shifted inside him over the past few years?

No, he couldn't weaken now. He knew what he had to do. Grabbing her suitcase, he made his way out the front door. She stood for a moment, her hand pressed to her mouth, then she gathered her strength and followed him.

She wasn't going to cry. She couldn't cry. She couldn't let him see her that weak. She was sorry she'd come on that strong, but she'd meant every word of it. It hadn't changed his mind, but then, what could? Janie didn't have to fight for him. She already had him. She always would.

As she made her way through his living room, her gaze fell on the snowy paperweight, and without thinking, her hand closed on it and dropped it into her purse. "Maybe I'll steal something," she'd told him on the first night. "Then you could arrange to have me arrested and bring me back here."

Fat chance. He didn't want her back here. But she would have a souvenir. Something to remember him by.

She stood watching him stow her bag in the trunk, clinging to every detail, storing it away for later. She had no picture of him. This was all she would ever have, so she knew she needed to keep it all clear and real.

Closing the trunk, he turned to face her, and she lifted her arms, surrendering to the need to hold him one more time.

He took her to him and held her close, his face buried in her hair. She closed her eyes and took him all in, every feeling, every scent, every sound.

I love you, she thought. But she couldn't say it aloud. What would be the use? He couldn't respond in kind. He couldn't let himself. To say something like that to her, to mean it, would be a betrayal of his love for Janie.

"Goodbye," she whispered instead, fighting back the tears. "Stay well."

Turning, she stumbled away from him and flung herself into the car. She started the engine quickly, not looking at him, and turned out onto the road. Only when she was a fair distance from the house did she look into the rearview mirror. He was still standing there, watching her go. And that was when the tears finally came.

The drive was a long one, but she hardly noticed it. Her mind was filled with emotions that kept her churning for hours. Just days before, she'd approached going to this baby shower with a mixture of joy and dread—joy in seeing her old friends again, dread in seeing Sara with child when she knew that would only point out to her the emptiness of her life without a baby. And now things were so different. Now she was rushing toward the shower to find comfort with her friends, and rushing away from the man that she loved and could never have. Life was certainly odd. And unpredictable.

She pulled into a motel and booked a room, but she couldn't eat and she sat in front of the television set and never saw the picture. Her mind was racing. What could she do to convince Rafe that he needed her?

Nothing, she decided at last. If a man couldn't see that for himself, there was no way to change his mind.

Still, she couldn't stop thinking. She formulated plans to revamp his entire sheriff's office and show him how much use she could be to him. She decided the sheriff's station ought to be the center of activity for the entire town. She could supervise setting up youth programs and other things to teach people skills. For instance, if someone were to run a magazine right there in the little town, they could hire people and teach them editing, layout, using a computer, printing—all that. Someone with, say, a fern journal.

The possibilities were endless. Darn it, who needed the city, anyway? There were horizons of opportunity she'd never dreamed of in Rafe's town.

But what was the use of thinking about it? He would never invite her back there. He'd liked her a lot. She could tell that. But he'd felt guilty about it, and he didn't want to feel that way. So he'd sent her on and told her not to come back. The happiness they could make together wasn't worth the pain to him. And that was just the way it was going to have to be.

She wasn't going to think about it any longer. Now if only she could get her eyes to stop staring so hard at the ceiling, maybe she could get some sleep.

Rafe was just as bad, prowling the office, barking at Sam, snapping at people on the phone. Nothing was good enough for him, and no one was allowed to say anything to him without getting a short-tempered answer.

"You miss Cami, don't you?" Sam said to him at one point.

"The hell I do," he retorted, but the wave of sadness that swept over him told him he was a liar, and he had to grit his teeth to keep from letting a picture of the way she'd looked in the snow settle into his mind.

A group of children stopped by the office. At first he assumed they were looking for the lady prisoner, but to his surprise, it turned out they just wanted to see him, watch him work. They followed him as he made his rounds of the little town. He felt like the Pied Piper with the string of kids straggling behind wherever he went. They watched, wide-eyed, as he strapped on his holster and got into his blue-and-white to head up into the hills. He almost wished he could take them with him. They made him smile, despite everything.

But that was about the only thing that made him smile. By late afternoon, he'd about had enough of himself, and he looked up with a frown as Sam entered the office to help lock up.

"Hey, Rafe, old buddy," his friend said, greeting him with a king-size grin. "Guess what? I've got a date with Sally. A real, live date. We're going to drive down to Santa Fe for dinner and a show. And who knows what else, if my magnificent charm kicks into overdrive. You just never know."

Rafe had to hold back the sarcastic comment that rose to his lips. Somehow he didn't seem to be able to take any joy in someone else's happiness today.

"Good luck." He swallowed hard and made himself smile. "What made her change her mind about you?"

Sam shrugged happily. "She's finally over you." He slapped Rafe's shoulder. "Yup. That's what she told me."

"That's good news." And in fact, it actually was.

"Yeah, it is, isn't it? She said, after she saw the way you were with the blonde, she realized there was no use pining any longer."

That startled him. "What are you talking about?" he said, turning to look at his friend.

"Well, she said there's only one other person she's ever seen you look at that way. And that's that picture you keep of the woman you used to love. That gal down in L.A."

Rafe growled, frowning. "When did she ever see me…?"

"Oh, women have their ways," Sam said, brushing that aside with a wave of his hand. "They're always watching us. Didn't you know that? They see things we don't even know we're doing. They can read minds. They love that stuff." He shrugged his complete bewilderment over the nature of women. "Anyway, she says she realized, if you were going to let somebody walk out of your life who you felt like that about, there was no hope. So she gave up on you. She thinks you're hopeless." He chuckled. "Hey, man. You're hopeless. Got that?"

Sam left, whistling a happy tune, and Rafe stared after him.

He was hopeless. A hopeless fool. Sally was absolutely right. But there wasn't much he could do about it.

He locked up, casting a quick glance at the empty cell just before he left. Stopping at the market on the way home, he picked up some groceries to fill his refrigerator.

"As though," he told himself scornfully as he walked to his car with the sack of supplies, "she was coming back and you had to get ready for her. You *are* hopeless."

At the house, he rambled from one room to another, imagining he could still catch a hint of her scent in the air. Every place he looked had a memory of Cami floating in it. He built a roaring fire in the fireplace and sat watching it, his mind full of her, his senses numbed by the terrible loneliness without her. And then he couldn't stand it any longer. He put on his parka and went back to the office. At least there, most of the memories were of arguing, not lovemaking.

He found things to work on until well after midnight, and then, suddenly, he had a visitor.

"Hi." Sally peeked in, smiling at him. "Are you still working?"

"Yeah." He turned his bleary gaze on her and tried to smile back. "How was the date with Sam?"

She came on into the office, smiling secretively. "Okay. We had a good time."

"You're back kind of early, aren't you?"

She nodded. "I didn't want him to think he'd come too far quite so quickly," she confided. "It's best to plan these things ahead, you know."

Rafe laughed softly. "Poor old Sam. He doesn't know what he's in for."

"Oh, I think he has some idea. And if not, it's time he found out." She grinned, then turned back toward the door, glancing at him over her shoulder and pausing thoughtfully. "But it's not so bad. There's one advantage men always have—we women are in love with love. You know what I mean?"

He stared at her, not sure he really did.

She put her hand on the knob but didn't turn it. "We want people to be in love. We feel more comfortable when everyone has paired off." Her smile was full of genuine affection. She hesitated, then went on carefully. "Your...your Janie is the same, Rafe, I'm sure of it. She'd want you to love again. She'd consider it a tribute to the special relationship the two of you had together." She hesitated, then gave him an audacious wink. "Think about it, Sheriff. Just mull it over for a while." And with a swirl of her skirt, she was gone.

Rafe sat, staring after her, her words echoing in his head, but in a confusing maelstrom that didn't do much to clarify his mind at the moment. Then he noticed a piece of paper on the floor. Bending, he picked it up. It was the invitation to the baby shower Cami had been carrying in her pocket. Crumpling it, he pushed it into his own pocket. And then he locked up and went home.

It wasn't until he went to bed that he realized he'd spent the day thinking about Cami, not Janie. And for once, the black guilt didn't descend upon him. Instead, there was a warm feeling.

"Janie?" he whispered to the open air. There was no answer, but there was an enveloping feeling of peace, and in a moment, he drifted into a deep, deep sleep.

Cami forced herself out of bed and brushed her teeth and looked at the horrible aberration in her motel room mirror.

Was that red-eyed monster really her? She felt as though she hadn't slept at all—and she looked it, too. It was all Rafe's fault, and she was happy to lay it on his shoulders. What an infuriating man. She was better off without him.

But she knew she was bluffing, trying to fool herself. She loved him, for Pete's sake. And here she was driving away from him as fast as she could go.

She skipped breakfast and drove on, thinking furiously again, trying to find a way to resolve this dilemma. There had to be some way to make him see the light. But the harder she thought, the more hopeless it seemed. And when she finally pulled into Denver, she resolved to put those thoughts behind her. Her experience with Rafe was over. It had been a short respite from the real world, and now it was time to get back to reality.

Reality meant Sara and this baby shower. Here she was with her broken heart and her empty life, limping in to help Sara celebrate her own perfect existence. But hadn't it always been that way? Sara had always beat her out at everything. Like sisters, they'd loved each other dearly and competed like crazy—over grades, club offices, men—you name it, they'd vied to be the first. The rivalry had never been fierce, but it had always been there, a subtle subtext to their lives. Cami had been the instinctive competitor, the uncombed one, the late one, the one who relied on sudden inspiration. Sara had been the prepared one, the studied one, the one whose life was always as perfect as her hair.

And now she was the one having a baby. Cami wasn't jealous. Not exactly. At least, she was trying very hard not to be. But she wasn't in the best of moods as she cruised into Denver.

She had no trouble at all finding Sara's house. It stood out like a sore thumb—or maybe it would be more accurate to say it stood out like a diamond at a dime store counter. The place was perfect, of course. Would Sara have it any other way?

"It looks like Disneyland," Cami muttered to herself as she pulled up in front of it. "It looks like a thousand tiny workers toil ceaselessly all night, every night, to keep it perfect."

The house appeared like a small version of a modern fairy-tale castle, with turrets and balconies and twisting evergreens reaching for the sky. The storm had left a dusting of snow, adding to the magical qualities of the place. A long, sweeping driveway led up to the large oak entryway.

Cami drove up it and stopped, feeling relief to have made it, and a sense of her energy draining away. She was shaky as she got out of the car, and when a tall, blond woman ran out of the house, charging toward her, she braced herself, leaning against the fender.

The woman stopped a foot away, gazing at her open-mouthed. "Cami?" she said.

Cami blinked, peering against the sun. "Sara?" she said, shading her eyes. "Is that really you?"

"Yes!"

They embraced with all the exuberance of college girls again, laughing and holding tightly.

"You really came?"

"You didn't think I'd miss it, did you?"

"I can't believe you're really here."

"Oh, Sara." Cami sighed as the surge of adrenaline from their meeting began to recede. "I . . . I thought I'd never make it." Her voice trembled and suddenly her eyes were wet. She was just so tired, so spent. And she was afraid that once the tears started flowing, she wouldn't be able to stop crying. "This is ridiculous," she murmured to herself, dabbing at her eyes.

Sara gave her another hug. "Hey. You can't be that happy to see me."

"I'm not." She sniffed, and grabbed another tissue from her purse. "I mean, of course I'm happy to see you, but that's not why . . ."

Sara pulled her close and dropped a kiss on her cheek. "You've had an adventure, haven't you? Something's happened. Well, you'll have to tell me all about it."

"Later. When I have the energy."

Grabbing the suitcase Cami was fumbling with, Sara began to lead her into the house, looking down at her old friend and frowning.

"You look like…you know, I hate to say it, but you look like hell."

"I know. I feel like I've been through hell to get here." She sighed again. "Is there someplace I could go and lie down for a while before I meet your friends?"

"Sure."

She led her into the house, chattering as they went, but Cami didn't take in much of it. She was in a daze. She did note that the house was decorated wonderfully for the shower. On their way to the stairs, they passed an enormous stuffed bear beside the equally large stuffed giraffe that guarded the entry to the kitchen. The table was piled high with pink packages sporting puffy white bows. Pink and white streamers were draped gracefully over every doorway. Pink and white balloons bobbed in groups of three or five. Pink and white icing gleamed on the silky white cake, icing so thick, you could drown in it.

"Wow," Cami said weakly as they kicked aside the pink confetti to get to the foot of the stairs. She looked up at the small white, fuzzy teddy bears that hung from the ceiling. "It looks like someone is going to have a baby shower today."

She turned to smile at her old friend, but the smile froze on her face as she realized something that didn't jibe with the occasion. "Hey," she said, startled by the revelation. "You're not pregnant." She stared at Sara in bewilderment. "Did you already have the baby?"

Sara's face took on a strained look. "It's a long story, Cam, and you're much too tired to sit through it. I'll tell you all about it later.'' She opened the door to a bedroom and drew her inside. "You get some rest. I'll get you up in time for the shower."

And she disappeared, leaving Cami behind, still frowning. Something was definitely wrong, but she couldn't deal with it right now. She was just too exhausted.

She took a quick shower, put on the flowing white nightgown that she had brought along for the occasion and slipped between the exquisite sheets. She was asleep before her head hit the pillow, and she slept for hours. Sara looked in on her a time or two, but she had her own concerns getting ready for the shower, and as noon crept into afternoon, Cami was alone.

She woke with a start, as though something had touched her, but when she looked around the room, there was nothing there. But she was fully awake now, awake and refreshed. As she lay, looking out the window at the trees outside, their deep green branches tipped with snow, she thought of Rafe and wondered if she'd dreamed it all.

Music was playing downstairs. And as she lay there, she began to make out voices from below. The shower! How late was it?

Scrambling out of bed, she found the clock. The shower had just begun. If she worked quickly, she could get down and join in before she was really missed. She found the pink wool suit she'd brought to wear and laid it out, then reached into her hair, wondering what she was going to do to tame it.

But at the same time, her gaze was caught by something out in the backyard. Someone was moving among the trees. Curiously she opened the French doors to the balcony and leaned out into the chilly air, searching the snowy greenery.

There. Something moved behind the gazebo. And there it was again. Someone was coming down the hill into the yard, making his way through the trees, someone tall and dark and handsome. She blinked hard, trying to focus. Was she dreaming, or what?

Rafe was pushing his way through the bushes and swearing as his sleeve tore on a thorn. If he'd stopped to think about it, he would have felt like a perfect fool, but he didn't have time for that. He had to find Cami.

He'd woken before dawn and knew what he had to do the moment his eyes had opened. Cami was right. Sally was right. Everyone was right, everyone except for him and his very annoying conscience. He hadn't fallen in love that often in his life. It had happened with Janie, and he'd lost her before their life together had even really begun. Now it had happened again with Cami. How could he let her walk away? He knew he had to see her again. They hadn't known each other long enough to be sure, but he'd known her long enough to know this was probably the best chance for happiness he would ever have. He couldn't let it slip away.

He'd been driving ever since, racing along the highway, heart beating and nerves fraying. And now here he was, skulking around the edges of the damn baby shower, trying to find the woman he very possibly might be in love with.

His breath was coming out in small, misty clouds, and he was maneuvering carefully, so as not to be seen by the women gathering inside the house. He could see them all, beyond the covered swimming pool, through the glassed-in terrace, into the living room. The shower seemed to be in full swing. The women were milling about, holding cups and talking to one another. Now just how was he going to pick Cami out of the crowd and get her attention without anyone else seeing him?

"Rafe?"

He looked around quickly.

"Up here!" she directed.

He heard her and looked up. There she was, on a white balcony in a flowing white gown. Just as though it were meant to be. He grinned, looking at her. "Hi," he said, saluting her.

She breathed quickly, hardly believing it at first. "Rafe!" She flung herself all the way out into the cold air, leaning over the railing of the balcony. Her heart was thumping like a drum gone berserk. Rafe. It couldn't be. It was just too magical to find him out wandering among the enchanted trees. But there he was. And the next thing she knew, he was right below where she stood, testing the strength of the lathe work laid against the side of the house, looking for a vine that was currently dormant.

"What are you doing?" she whispered loudly.

He glanced up at her. "I'm coming up," he said, and as she watched with a mixture of horror and delight, he did just that, coming hand over hand up the trellis, until he vaulted over the railing and into her arms.

She laughed as he covered her face with kisses, drawing him into the room and closing the doors. "What are you doing here?" she cried, gazing at him with pure delight.

"It's all in the line of duty, ma'am," he told her. "I'm afraid I'm obligated to arrest you again."

Her face fell. "What are you talking about?"

His hand curled around the back of her head. "You walked off with my paperweight, didn't you? That's burglary."

She laughed aloud. "Another accusation! Prove it, Mr. Lawman."

He pulled her close, holding her a prisoner in his arms, looking down into her face with all his emotion bared. But his voice remained light and playful. "I know you've got it on you. Nobody else would have taken it."

She stared up at him, hoping what she was reading in his eyes was the truth. "Circumstantial evidence," she murmured. "It won't hold up in court."

He dropped another kiss on her mouth. "We'll see about that."

She laughed softly, wonderingly. "Do you mean to tell me you came all this way for that?"

"Sure. I told you I'd come and arrest you if you stole something from me."

"But that was supposed to be next Christmas."

"I couldn't wait that long."

She could hardly breathe. Was he really saying what she thought he was saying? "Why not?"

He held her closer and his voice lowered. "Because I couldn't go without you in my arms for that long," he murmured, nuzzling her ear.

Her heart stopped, then started again, racing wildly. "Rafe..."

Drawing back, he looked down at her earnestly. "Cami, I need you. I can't help it." He shrugged, looking helpless. "I... I got hooked, and I can't let you go."

Words couldn't do the job of expressing how she felt, so she let her body give it a try. His hands dispensed with the white gown as though it were made of morning dew, clearing the way to her warm, rounded flesh, and she slipped her own hands beneath his heavy sweater, thirsting for the feel of his hard, muscular form. There was no hesitation between them any longer. They'd known each other such a short time, and yet they knew each other so well. They came together as though they had been born for this, had waited for it all their lives. It was real, right and splendid between them. She ached for him, took him in and gloried in his tenderness. He hungered for her, took her, and was astounded by her uninhibited joy in their lovemaking. Neither of them had ever experienced anything like it. They were unique in all the world, and they were breathless with the wonder of it.

"We could make a baby this way, you know," she warned him as they caught their breath.

He captured her mouth with his own and kissed her, hard. "You deserve a baby," he whispered very near her ear.

"What?'' She turned her head, looking for his eyes, wanting to read his meaning.

"I said you deserve a baby.''

She laughed softly. "Yes, but my baby deserves a father. That's the only way it can be.''

"You're right,'' he said softly, tracing a line between her breasts to her navel with his index finger. "You deserve that, too.''

"What?'' She wished he would look at her so she could see into his eyes. She twisted, trying to get a better look. "What did you say?''

He took a handful of her hair and pressed it to his lips, but before he could answer a burst of song from below interrupted them, tearing them away from this fantasy of love and returning them to reality.

"The shower,'' he reminded her, jackknifing away.

"Oh, God, the shower.'' She jumped up, as well. "You've got to get out of here. I've got to go down to join them.''

"Okay. I'll go.'' He touched her cheek lovingly. "But I'm coming back.''

Her heart was full, but she didn't dare ask any questions. He'd said some very provocative things, but she didn't take anything for granted. She slipped into the pink wool suit, her mind in a whirl, while he pulled on his jeans and sweater and went back out on the balcony.

"See you tonight,'' he whispered, giving her one last, crooked smile, and then he stepped over the edge.

He'd barely disappeared from sight when she heard the laughter begin. Rushing to the balcony, she looked down to see Rafe clinging to the trellis, and a roomful of women crowding out onto the glassed-in terrace to watch his descent. They were all there, and they were all witnesses to the fact that Rafe was leaving her in a nontraditional way.

"Don't give it a second thought,'' Sara called out above the giggles, raising her cup of punch to Cami with laughter in her eyes. "I'm sure it's just the plumber, come to check the water pressure."

Cami gazed down at Rafe in horror, sure he must be mortified. But to her surprise, he landed gracefully on his feet and turned to make a deep bow to the ladies watching.

"Not really," he told them calmly. "Actually, I'm Rafe Lonewolf, come to ask Cami Bishop to marry me."

There was a startled, frozen moment of shocked stillness. Then a collective sigh escaped the crowd.

"What did she say?" someone called out.

Rafe grinned, glancing up at where Cami was staring down, her face white, her mouth agape. "I haven't got up the nerve to actually ask her yet. But when I do..."

"When he does," Cami called down, shaking her head, still in shock, "I... I want you all to be the first to know, I think I'm going to say yes."

A cheer rose from the crowd, and Rafe turned to meet Cami's wondering gaze.

"I love you," he mouthed to her.

Leaning over the rail, she blew him a kiss. "I love you, too," she said aloud. "Now, and forever."

The shower ladies cheered and Rafe turned and saluted them gallantly, then strode off toward where his car was parked.

"Hey," Sara called up to her friend. "When I invited you to my baby shower, I didn't know you were going to bring along part of the entertainment."

"Neither did I," Cami said, then whispered it again to herself as she retreated into the room to continue dressing for the shower. "Neither did I."

She looked in the mirror. Just days ago, she'd been driving on her way to this shower, feeling glum and left out of life. Now there was love, a wedding, and babies in her future. She smiled, feeling the glow that was sure to show in her eyes from now on.

I wonder if he'll let me call him Reginald? she mused, then laughed aloud. The answer to that one was no, and she knew it without having to ask. But she didn't care. She had everything she wanted.

With a sigh of pure joy, she turned on her heel and headed for the stairs, on her way to join in the celebration of babies and newborn love.

*   *   *   *   *

If you liked BABY DREAMS, don't miss the next instalment in Raye Morgan's THE BABY SHOWER series coming in February 1997 from Silhouette Desire®.

MILLS & BOON®

Weddings ✤ *Glamour* ✤ *Family* ✤ *Heartbreak*

Weddings By DeWilde

✤

Since the turn of the century, the elegant and fashionable DeWilde stores have helped brides around the world realise the fantasy of their 'special day'.

Now the store and three generations of the DeWilde family are torn apart by the separation of Grace and Jeffrey DeWilde—and family members face new challenges and loves in this fast-paced, glamourous, internationally set series.

For weddings, romance and glamour, enter the world of

Weddings By DeWilde

—a fantastic line up of 12 new stories from popular Mills & Boon authors

NOVEMBER 1996

Bk. 3 DRESSED TO THRILL - Kate Hoffmann
Bk. 4 WILDE HEART - Daphne Clair

Available from WH Smith, John Menzies, Volume One, Forbuoys, Martins, Woolworths, Tesco, Asda, Safeway and other paperback stockists.

♦™ SILHOUETTE

Desire

COMING NEXT MONTH

THE ACCIDENTAL BODYGUARD Ann Major

Man of the Month

The last thing lawyer Lucas Broderick wanted to do was protect the gorgeous woman he found hiding in his house. But she'd lost her memory…and now Lucas was losing his heart…

FATHER OF THE BROOD Elizabeth Bevarly

Sexy playboy Ike Guthrie reluctantly sold himself in a bachelor auction and was accidentally won by Annie Malone. Could the confirmed bachelor and the mother of a brood of children share more than a wild attraction?

THE GROOM, I PRESUME? Annette Broadrick

Daughters of Texas

Maribeth O'Brien was everything Chris Cochran wanted in a woman. So when she was left at the altar by her would-be groom, Chris stepped in to say, 'I do'!

FALCON'S LAIR Sara Orwig

Ben Falcon knew there was only one reason for a beautiful woman to have invaded his remote ranch. But until the mystery woman regained her memory, he could pretend she was someone he could trust - and that he was someone she could love…

HARDEN Diana Palmer

Texan Lovers

Rugged Harden Tremayne was the toughest, wildest man ever to come out of Texas. Miranda Warren had never felt anything as overwhelming as her passion for the long, lean cowboy. But was her love enough to melt his hard, hungry heart?

THE PRODIGAL GROOM Karen Leabo

The Wedding Night

Laurie Branson had been devastated when irresistible Jake Mercer left her at the altar. Now he was back—and that meant she had to keep a three-year-old secret she'd hidden since he left.

COMING NEXT MONTH FROM

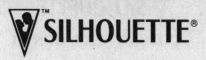
SILHOUETTE®

Sensation

*A thrilling mix of passion, adventure
and drama*

UNCERTAIN ANGELS Kim Cates
ONE GOOD MAN Kathleen Creighton
CUTS BOTH WAYS Dee Holmes
SERIOUS RISKS Rachel Lee

Intrigue

Danger, deception and desire

RECKLESS LOVER Carly Bishop
EXPOSÉ Saranne Dawson
MIDNIGHT COWBOY Adrianne Lee
BABY VS. THE BAR M.J. Rodgers

Special Edition

Satisfying romances packed with emotion

PART-TIME WIFE Susan Mallery
THE REBEL'S BRIDE Christine Flynn
MARRIAGE-TO-BE? Gail Link
WAITING AT THE ALTAR Amy Frazier
RESIST ME IF YOU CAN Janis Reams Hudson
LONESOME COWBOY Lois Faye Dyer

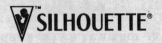

Dark Secrets...
Dangerous Desires

Don't miss this superb three in one collection
featuring thrilling love stories with an edge of
darkness, suspense and paranormal, from some
of Silhouette's best-loved authors...

Heather Graham Pozzessere
Anne Stuart
Helen Myers

Available: October 1996   Price: £4.99

To celebrate the **1000**th Desire™ title we're giving away a year's supply of Silhouette Desire® novels — absolutely *FREE!*

All you have to do is complete the puzzle below and send it to us by 31 December 1996.

The first 10 correct entries drawn from the bag will each win 12 month's free supply of seductive and breathtaking Silhouette Desire books (6 books every month—worth over £160). The second correct 10 entries drawn will each win a Silhouette music cassette.

S
E
N
S
U
O
U
S

Word	Letters
SENSUOUS	8
DESIRE	6
DARING	6
SEDUCTIVE	9
EMOTIONAL	9
COMPELLING	10
PASSIONATE	10
CAPTIVATING	11
ADVENTUROUS	11
PROVOCATIVE	11

Please turn over for entry details

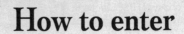

CELEBRATION 1000

How to enter

There are ten words listed overleaf, each of which fits into spaces in the grid according to their length. All you have to do is fit the correct word into the appropriate spaces that have been provided for its letters. We've even done the first one for you!

When you have completed the grid, don't forget to fill in your name and address in the space provided below and pop this page into an envelope (you don't even need a stamp) and post it today. Hurry—competition ends 31st December 1996.

**Silhouette® Words of Love
FREEPOST
Croydon
Surrey
CR9 3WZ**

Are you a Reader Service Subscriber?   Yes ☐   No ☐

Ms/Mrs/Miss/Mr _____

Address _____

_____

_____ Postcode _____

One application per household.

You may be mailed with other offers from other reputable companies as a result of this application. If you would prefer not to receive such offers, please tick box. ☐

mps MAILING PREFERENCE SERVICE   **DMA**   SILC96